W9-AEE-610

CHASING CHARLIE

CHASING CHARLIE

•

Kathy Carmichael

AVALON BOOKS
NEW YORK

PRINTED IN THE UNITED STATES OF AMERICA
ON ACID-FREE PAPER
BY HADDON CRAFTSMEN, BLOOMSBURG, PENNSYLVANIA

This book is dedicated to the special people who helped me
make my dream a reality:
Debby Mayne, my extraordinary editor, Erin Cartwright,
Jan Nickols of the Clearwater Public Library System,
my mother, Charlotte Lynch Nohr, and
sisters Paula, Robin, Karla and Terri.

And always and forever to John, Andrew and Ian, who love
me despite the fast food.

Acknowledgments

My sincerest gratitude to those who've helped and encouraged me: Val Daniels, Susan Fox, Vicki Hinze, Julie Leto, Carollyn Stringer, Libby Sydes, the Goddesses of X-Romex and the Sandies: Susan Carter, Rebecca Cox, Jea Dudley and Karen Fox.

Words cannot express what I owe each of the Trolls: Joanne Barnes, Carla Cassidy, Ali Cunliffe, Lynn Harris, Avis Hester, Trish Jensen, Terry Kanago, Judy Miller, Michelle Miller, Hannah Rowan, Beth Stegenga, RaeAnne Thayne and John "Ogre" Helwig.

Thank you all.

Chapter One

It was love at first sight. Charlotte Nelson rocked back on her heels, closed her eyes a moment and then reopened them. There was no doubt about it. She'd fallen in love—with a dress.

"How'd you like to try *that* on for size?" asked the sales clerk, stepping up behind her.

"I'm just looking." Charlie sighed, casting one last longing look at the clingy red dress before replacing it on the rack.

The girl emitted a low sigh. "Me, too."

"Oh, I don't know. I've never tried anything like that before." If she wore it, what would the neighbors think? But the feeling the dress evoked was palpable. Maybe the clerk had a point. "Does it come in black?"

1

"The hat?"

What hat? Charlie gave the clerk a double-take.

"I wouldn't change a thing." The clerk was positively drooling and her eyes were trained on . . . something other than the dress. Or rather, *someone*.

Oh no. Not the Rhinestone Cowboy.

Charlie recognized him immediately, the Rhinestone Cowboy who frequented her library research department. He'd soaked up more books on cowboys and ranching than anyone she'd ever met. "I don't *do* cowboys," Charlie said.

"My gain." After watching him until he was out of sight, the sales clerk grinned, then gestured toward the dress. "Red is your color. You ought to try it on."

"You think so?" Charlie bit her lip. Normally she wore muted colors, more fitting for her job as a librarian. She wore sensible fabrics: cottons, synthetic blends and wools. Certainly, nothing like this—the personification of everything she'd like to be and couldn't.

But what about the lecture from her roommate, Joanne? Was it time for her to let loose a little? Joanne certainly seemed to feel that way. In fact, she'd called Charlie a turtle, hiding from the world.

She ran her forefinger down the satiny smoothness of the fabric. How she wanted to be the type of woman who could wear a dress like this. She searched her memory for something, anything, she might own that felt so deliciously different, and came up empty.

"Go ahead and try it on," encouraged the clerk, nodding with perky enthusiasm, as if a dress could repair all that ailed Charlie.

Joanne had said the reason Charlie felt isolated was because she'd set herself up to feel that way, by withdrawing from life. She hadn't withdrawn, not exactly. But if she put her heart out there, she risked being hurt—again. She risked that feeling of somehow never doing it "right," of never being able to measure up, of somehow lacking some essence that others seemed to carry confidently on their shoulders.

The dress might prove to Joanne and herself that she could. She'd start small, though. She'd experiment a little, take a few more risks like the satiny red dress. She nodded at the clerk who quickly snapped up the dress and led her back to the dressing rooms.

Charlie normally didn't shop at Neiman's and she'd never visited the dressing rooms before. They were larger than in most stores, with a chair and a real door. Soon she was alone behind the closed door and there was nothing in the room to look at save the mirror, the chair and The Dress.

She quickly stepped out of her neat lavender

shirtwaist and laid it across the chair. Then she pulled the red dress off the hanger and slid it over her head. As if it had been custom made for her, it clung to her hips and hugged her form. Was that *her* in the mirror, looking excited and a little guilty?

She started at the sound of a knock on the door. Opening it a crack, the clerk peeked her head in. "Come out here and look at yourself in the full-length mirrors."

Before Charlie had time to refuse, the clerk was pulling her to the mirrors.

"It's perfectly lovely, and fits you like a dream."

There, before Charlie's eyes, were three images of herself, and she looked as poised as any magazine cover model. She looked like a woman who gulped life, didn't measure it in risks taken. Was it her imagination, or did the very air around her crackle with excitement? The woman gazing back at her looked as though she was the life of every party, not the wallflower watching from a dark corner. No, this woman didn't know dark corners existed. Could a dress do all that?

Oh, I couldn't, she argued with her little voice. But the voice was insistent.

This dress should prove to Joanne, and to herself, that she was a risk-taker. Sure, she didn't take heedless chances, but the occasional rash purchase was perfectly within her capacity. What had really stung was when Joanne accused her of not changing toothpaste brands, or flavors, since 1986—and it had been true. She couldn't remember ever using another product. She'd immediately gone out and bought three other brands but hadn't tried them yet.

Joanne had been right. But not anymore.

"I'll take it."

"All I want is to be a cowboy," said R. Davis Murphy to Jim Turner, long-term family friend and boyfriend of Davis's widowed mother. The candy department of the store wasn't nearly as crowded and congested as the rest of Neiman's, and the aroma of chocolate was enticing. But Davis was here on a mission to select Valentine's Day gifts, and Jim had come along to pick out something for Davis's mother.

Davis picked up a chocolate cowboy hat stuffed with a popcorn bull and red foil candy hearts. "Not only do I want to be a cowboy, I want five—better make it six—of these hats. Don't want Bambi to feel left out."

Jim silently shook his head. His tall, thin frame looked as out of place in a candy department as a calf would look in a pen of bulls. "Aren't you ready to step away from Murphy Title yet?"

"You bet." Davis was more than ready. For the past eight years, he'd been wearing a Brooks Brothers suit and silk tie instead of the Resistol hat and jeans he craved, affixing his name to contracts instead of putting his brand on cattle. When his father had died, leaving Davis and his mother nearly destitute, the only asset they'd had was Murphy Title. Davis had stepped in, and after years of hard-learned lessons and even harder work, made it profitable enough so that it could run itself.

The time for pursuing his lifelong dream, to be a cowboy like his grandfather, had finally arrived. "I promoted Lily to president last week. There'll be a transition period while she gets up to snuff, and then I'm out of there. In the meantime, I've put a few calls in to real estate brokers."

"I'm sure the perfect ranch is out there waiting for you. You've made your mother and all of us proud, Davis. It's good to know you'll soon be doing something for yourself. I'd hate to head off to Tokyo and think of you working at a job you don't enjoy." Jim leaned close to the glass counter, checking out the selection of truffles. "You know, if I'd had my way, you wouldn't have had to worry about money. But your mother wasn't willing to accept my charity then, and still isn't ready for anything more."

Davis patted Jim on the back. It wasn't any wonder his mother and Jim had fallen in love. And Jim's job transfer to Japan would take place in only two weeks. Who knew when he'd ever be back? "Knowing you were there made it all possible."

The older man waved away Davis's gratitude. "You and your mother are all the family I have."

"All you need is the perfect Valentine's gift to convince Mom to go to Japan with you," said Davis.

"You know, I've proposed more times than I can count, and she's always turned me down. I finally realized she's not going to marry me until you're safely settled."

Davis froze. A momentary shame washed over him. Mom was holding back because of him? Had he been so caught up in running the business that he hadn't been paying attention when he should have?

Jim seemed to know exactly the direction Davis's thoughts had run, because he cringed. "I shouldn't have said that."

Davis chewed it around in his mind. "You're right, though." His mother was very much in love with Jim. What else but worry over her only son would keep her from getting married?

His mother had sacrificed a lot for him. She wouldn't leave Davis alone, not after how she'd felt so alone after his father had died. It was time for him to return the favor. If she wanted to see him settled so that she'd feel free to marry the man she loved, then Davis owed it to her to make it possible.

Although there wasn't much time, there had to be a way to pull it off.

He ran his hand through his hair, thinking over the women he'd been dating. Although they were all attractive, enjoyable women, he couldn't work up anything more than a mild interest in any one of them—which explained the identical Valentine's gifts. He wasn't ready to marry someone simply for the sake of his mother's happiness.

But . . . what if he pretended to be engaged? His mother would feel free to marry the man she loved. "How about if I introduce her to my fiancée? Think that would do it?"

Jim started, then dourly eyed the six chocolate hats Davis had lined up on the counter. "Why haven't we heard anything about her until now? Who is she?"

"I'm not sure yet. The women I've been seeing won't do." Davis shook his head, thoroughly swept up by the idea. "No, I need a woman who'll understand it's just a temporary engagement."

Two weeks. Surely any woman would agree to be engaged to him for two weeks. "And she'd darn well better be one Mom finds acceptable, or else she'll never run off with you."

"Forget it, Davis." Jim shot him a stern look. "You can't come dragging home some woman simply to trick your mother."

"You said yourself that Mom won't marry you until I'm settled. I'm not ready to settle down yet—I'm still too busy trying to buy my ranch—but I can at least give her this, Jim. Mom deserves to be happy."

"You're crazy. This isn't the way to go about it. Eventually your mother will come around."

"Yeah, and I get to watch her mope with heartache while you're having the time of your life in Tokyo. No. I just have to find the right woman."

"You already have more women than you know what to do with. This isn't a good idea."

Davis waved away Jim's misgivings. He wracked his brain, trying to think of someone who would fit not just his but his mother's requirements for an ideal mate. The harder he thought, the larger the blank. His jaw clenched. There had to be *someone* out there. "Another thing, it's got to be someone I'm attracted to. Otherwise, Mom would catch on that I'm not serious."

Bouncing dark gold curls drew his attention, framing the face of a woman who could only be described as cute, right down to the single dimple he could see from fifty feet away. He started to dismiss her, then recognition hit. "Hey, I know her."

Jim turned to look. "Who is she?"

"She's a librarian . . ." Davis threw some money on the counter.

"Come down to earth, Davis. You can't do this."

"And I bet she's single. Finish paying for these, okay? I'll see what I can do and catch up with you at the office."

"Hey, where do you think you're—"

Abruptly, Davis cut him off. "I'm not doing this for you. I'm doing it for Mom." Davis turned and dashed after the blond. He was certain he knew the woman's name . . . Nelson. Charlotte Nelson. That was it. He'd seen it often enough on her name tag. She was smart and surprisingly good-looking for a librarian. She was *exactly* the type of woman a man brought home to meet his mother.

He crossed the crowded aisles to catch up with her. "Miss Nelson?"

She stopped and turned.

"Miss Nelson, er, Charlotte?" Davis soon joined her. "This is the first time I've seen you outside the library."

She laughed. "I assure you even librarians have lives." She gazed directly at him.

Davis was struck by the richness of her hazel eyes. Not green, or blue, or brown, but some intriguing mixture of the three. He felt as if staring into her eyes was like looking into a kaleidoscope. Why hadn't he noticed before? Maybe the lighting at the library was different from the mall. Mentally

shaking himself, he said, "Could I buy you a cap-
puccino or coffee or something?"

She shook her head, sending her burnished gold
curls into motion. "My lunch hour is almost over
and I need to get back to work."

She was perfect, not beautiful in any conventional
way, but pretty and natural and cute. She held a red
dress on a hanger, wrapped in plastic. "That looks
heavy. Can I carry it for you?"

Actually it looked pretty daring for a librarian to
wear. Charlotte Nelson would be a knockout in it.
When she looked hesitant, he added, "Maybe I
could call you for a date?"

Charlie had one rule in life: the words *cowboy*
and *date* did not go together, no matter how cute
the cowboy.

Too bad he wasn't cute. No—Davis Murphy was
downright gorgeous.

He was the type that turned women's heads, fan-
tasies running through their minds. She had to stop
thinking like this. Turning to go, she said, "I think
I can handle this *heavy* dress by myself. I'll see you
at the library. Bye!"

She dashed toward the exit. When he'd first begun coming to the library, she'd been rather intrigued by his looks. Dark hair, trim physique, and
eyes so dark you could lose yourself in them. He'd
made her heart race until he asked where to find

information about purchasing farm equipment. Her interest had instantly chilled when she realized he was only interested in one subject, the subject she liked least in the world.

She heard him call out, "Wait!" Lowering her head, she pretended not to hear. Some of the aura from the dress must have clung to her; good-looking men did not try to pick her up. She stepped up her pace and pulled the dress bag closer to her body.

She had to admit it was fun to feel attractive. Buying the dress made her feel like a risk-taker. And even though she'd never be interested in a cowboy, the dress was a start. She felt pleased with herself.

She saw Davis following her. Walking a bit faster, she headed for Sears because she'd parked her car outside that entrance.

Men. They weren't easily discouraged. Thank goodness she was a librarian—they had to be quiet in libraries. If men like her brothers, Monty Joe and Bobby Gray, stormed into her workplace giving her orders, she could legitimately tell them to shush. If only she could figure out a way to discourage Davis.

He called out, "Wait, please, Charlotte!"

She ignored him, hoping that once they were in the Sears store, she would lose him. She checked over her shoulder as she wended past Major Appliances. Between Sporting Goods and the Lighting department, she saw the cowboy, hot on her trail. Darn it—he was gaining on her.

Trotting now, she headed for Lingerie—that last bastion for women, a female stronghold. Only the very bravest of men ventured into such territory. She'd surely lose him there.

She rounded the corner, then darted down an aisle lined with boxes containing undergarments. Now, if only she could locate the dressing room, the man would never find her.

She scanned the row behind her and breathed a sigh of relief. He must have gotten lost when she led him through the men's department. She'd deliberately chosen a route near the button-fly jeans.

A flashy red teddy caught her attention. It was nearly the exact shade as her new dress. It hung on a circular rack of assorted other red items, all in celebration of Valentine's Day. Some garments sported red-dyed ostrich plumes, others had white feathers, and there were a few with sparkling glitter. Charlie grinned, wondering what type of woman bought these things.

Checking to be sure the Rhinestone Cowboy hadn't found her, she tossed her purse and dress bag over her shoulder, then caressed the soft teddy between her fingers. What would it feel like to wear something so obviously feminine? All her underthings ran on the side of practicality rather than esthetics.

Feeling as though she was on a risk-taking roll, she considered buying it. The image of Joanne's shocked face flashed into her mind, making her grin. As she pulled the garment from the rack, she noticed movement from the corner of her eye. Heck, Roy Rogers had picked up her trail. There was no time to find the dressing room now.

Without thought, she did what she'd done when she'd been seven years old and hiding from her brothers. She dived into the circular rack of teddies and ducked her head.

She waited for what seemed an eternity. Peeking through a few of the soft garments, she didn't see him. She took a deep breath, inadvertently sucking in a couple of the feathers.

"Achoo!"

Oh, heavens. Had she given herself away? Seconds passed. Nothing. Good, he must've gone or he'd have been on her faster than a wild chicken.

What was wrong with her, anyway? Why should she allow some over-testosteroned hulk to intimidate her? As she stooped to gather up her new dress and the teddy, the rack of undergarments abruptly parted with a chorus of clacks. There, staring down at her, was the cowboy in question, attired in his customary conservative suit and Tony Lama boots.

Her brothers had always told her that the best defense was a good offense. "Oh, this is just what· I was looking for." What else could she do but bluff her way out of the situation?

He offered a hand to help her. Ignoring it, she stepped out, realizing her face must match the scarlet-hued clothing in her hands. Not only had he followed her all over the mall, but he caught her humiliating herself as well.

"I hoped to talk to you," he said.

"I really need to get back to work."

"If *you* won't do it," he demanded, "where am I going to find a fiancée?"

"Huh?"

"A fiancée."

One of Dallas's most eligible bachelors needed a fiancée? A few months back, she'd read a magazine article on bachelors and he had made the Top Ten list. The article had gone on to disclose information about the many women he had dated and why he was such a challenge.

So, his explanation for why he was looking for a wife should be good, or at least entertaining. She could only presume it was an unusual pickup line. "I can tell you I'm not interested, but talk fast. You can have as long as it takes for me to pay for this. Then I have to go."

She hadn't intended to buy the teddy, but he'd

aroused her curiosity. She wasn't even sure it was the right size.

"I might need a little longer than that."

"I'm sorry, but it's all the time I have." She made her way to the center aisle and a bank of cash registers, determined not to give him an inch. In her experience, men always wanted ten miles.

"I'm Davis Murphy." He smiled, showing even, white teeth. "Can I have your phone number?"

"Nope." She rolled her eyes. "I have a rule against giving my number to men who accost me in lingerie departments."

A pleading expression flashed across his face. "But I need a fiancée."

"Why?" Charlie's turn to check out arrived, and she handed the teddy to the clerk, who rang up the purchase.

"I need a pretend fiancée, just for one night . . ."

So he wasn't looking for a wife. Paying the clerk, Charlie took her bag and stepped away from the counter.

". . . to go with me to a party and meet my mother . . ."

She looked at her watch.

"And that's it. Just a short-term engagement."

"I'm sure any number of women would jump at the chance," she said dryly.

Davis sighed. "I won't pretend there aren't plenty of women who'd love to help me out of this fix."

She shifted the hanger to her other hand. "Why me?"

"My mother wouldn't like them. You look like the type of woman who's smart enough to pull this off—to be my fiancée, that is."

Charlie blew her bangs out of her face. What was it about her that made men not think of her as their types? He hadn't said it, but it was in his tone. No reason to feel disappointed; it was what she'd come to expect. She wasn't *his* kind of woman—she was his mother's type.

She shook her head. "I'm sorry."

"One measly night? It's a party at the country club, and we could just dash in and out if you're having a bad time. The man my mother is in love with has been transferred out of the country, and she won't agree to marry him unless she thinks I'm settled. Then they'll be off to Tokyo in two weeks, with no one the wiser. I'll explain later that things didn't work out. But in the meantime, she'll be happy."

"When is this get-together?" At least his reasons for the deception appeared to be altruistic.

"Tomorrow night. Valentine's Day."

"I'm really sorry. I've already got plans." *Another boring evening with Philip.* Even he didn't seem too enthusiastic about their relationship. It was as stale as week-old bread, and probably as moldy.

"You don't know anyone who's smart and looks like you, do you?"

"There aren't many women as smart as I am who'd go out with a cowboy." She almost felt sorry for him as he turned pitiful brown puppy-dog eyes at her—almost. Somehow those eyes reminded her of her brothers' prize bull. "Good luck!"

Turning, she started toward the parking lot, but John Wayne wasn't about to let her go. Oh, no. That would be too much to ask. He tagged along beside her.

She stopped. "I'm sure you'll find someone perfect. So long."

Still, he didn't go away. *Sheesh, what was it going to take to get rid of him?*

"Is this man bothering you, ma'am?" Her prayers for deliverance were answered when a mall security guard stepped up to join them.

Chapter Two

"It's like I have a huge sign on my chest that says *not your type*," Charlie said as she poured milk into a glass, accidently sloshing it onto the counter.

"Men can be obtuse," said Joanne. "What did you say?"

Leaning over to grab a paper towel to clean up the mess, Charlie bumped her head on the cupboard. "Ow."

Joanne grabbed a sponge from the sink and wiped up the spill. Taking the carton from Charlie's hand, she filled the glass. "Go sit down and drink your milk. I have a feeling you're dangerous in a kitchen right now."

Charlie did as she was told, taking a seat on the bar stool on the other side of the kitchen pass-through. She watched Joanne as she made dinner. To keep costs down, the two of them took turns cooking. Joanne cooked sophisticated dishes, using gourmet recipes, combining unusual ingredients into something delicious.

She was good-hearted about Charlie's throw-it-together methods. Charlie was an *emotion* chef, specializing in comfort food, and often baked goodies when she felt down.

And this was one of those times. She felt a good old-fashioned chocolate meringue pie coming on at any time. And her normally placid friend, Joanne, had been known to knock people out of her way for a slice.

"I told Davis I have a date," Charlie commented between sips of milk. She snickered. "Just before security ran him off."

"But you just canceled your date with Philip."

Charlie shrugged.

"Isn't Davis the same good-looking guy who made your heart flutter when he first came into the library?"

"That was before I realized he was some Rhinestone Cowboy."

Joanne reached across the bar and took Charlie's hand. "I don't want to hurt your feelings, but I'm going to be bluntly honest. You know I care about you, right?"

Charlie nodded as Joanne released her hand then went back to slicing carrots. "I know."

"You're going after the wrong kind of man. For some reason, you're hiding, trying to stay safe. And safety can be great, but sometimes we need a little risk." Joanne made a few sword-like motions with her knife. "Men like a chase and a conquest, but you scare off any man who comes on to you, who attracts you."

Had she been doing that? Heading them off *before* the pass? There was every likelihood Joanne was right. "What do you advise?"

"Calling Davis and saying you can go out after all."

Charlie couldn't believe her ears. "You've got to be kidding."

"I'm totally serious. The man is good-looking, makes a great living and has asked you out. What more do you want?"

"But he's a *cowboy*. Or, at least, he wants to be."

"So the man isn't perfect. What man is?"

Charlie leapt from her stool, determined to cook that pie. What did she have to lose? The one thing she dreaded most was losing her heart to a cowboy.

"You don't understand." She detested cowboys. The ones you loved broke your heart; the ones you didn't, you itched to slap.

"I think I understand all too well," replied Joanne.

"You're scared to death. If a guy has the slightest odor of horse about him, you run like crazy. So you took up with a loser like Philip who'd never love you, or you, him. No wonder you're lonely."

"I've worked too hard to escape from a ranch. I won't—I can't—go back to living on one."

"When did Davis ask you to?" A delicate aroma filled the air as Joanne threw the vegetables into the frying pan.

She had a point. Charlie had been making a lifetime commitment out of one date, but that didn't change matters. She *was* beginning to take risks. "I bought that dress, didn't I? It proves I can be daring when I want to."

Joanne smiled. "You did good, sweetie."

"I'm lonely, but change can start small. And it sure doesn't have to begin by dating a cowboy."

"I know. It's just that with me getting married, I worry about you darting back into your turtle shell." Joanne sighed. "What if I'm not here to nag you?"

"It's not like you're moving to another state, but I promise to keep working on it." She didn't have much choice. She was lonely and feeling isolated already. With Joanne moving out soon and her brothers three hundred miles away, her support system was eroding to the point of extinction. Something had to give, and that something was her. "I hope you're done in the kitchen. It's time to make meringue."

Davis tilted his leather chair back from his desk and grinned. Charlotte Nelson was one cute librarian. Why hadn't he noticed before? When she said she already had plans for Valentine's, he'd seen the hesitation in her eyes. He didn't believe her for one minute. No one as pretty as she should plan on spending Valentine's alone—especially when he needed her help. There had to be some way to convince her to meet his mother.

Just then, Lily del Rietz, his new president, barged into his office without even knocking. Davis raised his brow, trying for a formidable look, but it did no good. She didn't back off, but that was Lily. She never did.

"When are you going to stop moping and sign off on those contracts?" Lily never beat about the bush either.

Davis shrugged. "I'm sure they're fine."

She ran a hand through her gray hair. "Since they're the first I've drawn up without your assistance, I'd like to be assured they're more than fine. And normally, you'd be combing through them, looking to find some nit to pick. So what's going on?"

Lily was a trooper, fifty years old and married to

Murphy Title in a way he'd never be. Davis was glad she'd been around to drive him nuts. Until now.

"Woman trouble."

"Ha. A playboy like you doesn't have woman trouble. Murphy Title isn't having financial trouble, that much I know. So what is it, really?"

"I met a woman and—" Davis felt sheepish. He had an image to maintain, and women just didn't say no to Davis Murphy, especially when he'd turned on the charm.

"Don't tell me you're slipping. I can see it all over your face. Finally, a woman with the brass to turn you down." She chortled and rubbed her hands together.

Davis glared at her, then sighed. "It's even worse than that. She's a librarian, Lily, and somehow, by tonight, I've got to convince her to be my fiancée."

She looked at him slowly, carefully. Davis tried his best to appear as if he were a man in love, but he wasn't sure if Lily could see through his act or not.

"I see," she said. "This is a woman who knows the alphabet and had the audacity to turn you down. The combination must be lethal to a guy who normally dates women named Bambi and Heather." Then she smiled. "It's about time, Davis. What can I do to help?"

"I don't think you can." He picked up the pen on his desk, and twiddled it in his fingers. "I thought about just showing up at her house tonight and sweeping her off her feet."

"That sounds like a great plan. What's stopping you?"

"I don't know her address."

"What's the name of this goddess of mystery and intrigue?"

Davis laughed. "Her name's Charlotte Nelson, and she's no goddess—more like an elf."

"This is good. An elf who knows the alphabet and won't go out with you. After all the women I tried to set you up with, I might have known you'd want a pixie rather than a fairy." She jumped from her chair. "I'll be right back."

Davis groaned as he watched her dart from the room. His personal life would soon be the talk of the office. Why couldn't he learn to keep his big mouth shut?

On the other hand, once his mother learned he planned to get married, it wouldn't hurt that there'd been a fair amount of office gossip. If, and that was a big *if*, he could somehow manage to talk Charlotte into going along with his scheme.

Lily came back into his office beaming a smile so huge Davis couldn't help but return it. "You look like a bull who's gotten in with the cows."

"Here's Charlie Nelson's address."

"Charlie? Her name's Charlotte."

"Well, when I called the head librarian, that's what she told me the girl goes by." Lily sighed melodramatically. "Ah, young love."

Davis took the slip of paper she offered him and scanned the address. "I don't know how you got this, but I owe you one, Lily."

"I want to meet her, that's all I ask."

"I'll do my best."

"Good. Now if you'll be so kind as to get your patoot back to work, maybe we can make some headway around here, too."

Charlie sneezed. Then she sneezed again. "What am I going to do with all these roses?" She wailed at Joanne.

Philip had sent them to her after she'd called and canceled their date for that night. It didn't matter how many flowers he sent, though; she wasn't going out with him anymore. She'd been certain he'd be as relieved as she was about not having to go through with it. And now the aromatic allergens. No matter how pretty they were or how sweet they smelled, she was still allergic to them. "Achoo!"

"Maybe if I put them in my room and close the door?" Joanne offered tentatively.

"Go right ahead. Otherwise, I'm throwing 'em out the window."

Joanne grabbed up the mop bucket filled to over-flowing with long-stemmed red pollen, quickly placed them in her room and closed the door. She opened the front door of the apartment and waved it back and forth, clearing the air.

"Thanks. That's better." Charlie grinned at her friend as she closed the door and came to take a seat by her in the living room.

Charlie grabbed a tissue and blew her nose again.

"So, are you going to rethink going out with him?" asked Joanne.

Charlie shrugged. "What's the point? We're never going to fall in love, and I keep nodding off when he gets on one of his rants about jolly old England. Staying home with a good video beats that any time."

"But what about that dress you bought? It's perfect for Valentine's."

She'd bought the dress for herself, not for Philip. "I'll wear it for my big date with HBO."

"Yeah, go put it on! I want to see it on you."

Charlie dashed to her bedroom and pulled the dress from her closet. It was gorgeous. She tossed off her baggy T-shirt and jeans, then found the red teddy where she'd hidden it in her drawer. If she was going to do it, she'd do it right.

First stepping into the teddy, she then drew the red dress over her head, excitement gradually building inside her.

Picking up her hairbrush, she swept her unruly curls into the best French twist she could manage, and pinned it in place. Then she looked down at her feet, feeling a lot like Cinderella after she'd lost her shoe. Sneakers wouldn't work; neither would her penny loafers nor her two-inch black pumps.

Never mind. Since she wasn't leaving the apartment, shoes didn't really matter, although she wished she could complete the image because Joanne was going to be truly surprised.

With the most prissy walk she could manage, she emerged from her bedroom. Joanne looked up and screamed.

"Charlie! I can't believe it!" Joanne ran closer and looked her up and down. "I had no idea you had all those curves."

Charlie laughed. "I don't think I do, but this dress sure makes mountains out of molehills, doesn't it?"

Joanne nodded. "I wish I had molehills like those. Wow." Then she caught sight of Charlie's bare feet and an impish look entered her eyes. "I'll be right back."

Joanne made a beeline for her bedroom and came out carrying a shoe box as if it held the crown jewels. She handed the box to Charlie.

Pulling up the lid and pushing past the tissue, Charlie saw the deadliest-looking stiletto heels she'd ever seen in her life. "Where'd you find these, 'Madame's Bordello of Love'?"

Joanne flashed an embarrassed grin. "It was one of those buying binges. Once I got them home, I realized I didn't have anything to go with them. We're the same size, try them on!"

They looked lethal, but before Charlie could figure out how to decline Joanne's exuberant offering, the doorbell rang. For once, she'd been saved by the bell.

"That must be Mike." Joanne checked the wall clock as she headed for the door. "He's awfully early. I'm not even dressed yet."

"He probably couldn't last another moment out of your company. It's been nearly twenty hours since he saw you." Charlie pirouetted, enjoying the feel of the satin against her skin.

"Yeah, right. And once he sees you in that, he may forget all about his poor little fiancée." She pulled open the door.

"Oh, Philip, uh, come in." She stepped back and swung the door wider, sending Charlie a questioning look.

Charlie gulped. What the dickens was Philip doing here, anyway? She'd made it clear she wasn't going out with him tonight, or ever again for that matter.

Philip stalked confidently into the apartment, then caught sight of Charlie and stopped dead in his tracks. For the first time, Charlie saw a man's eyes boggle.

It must be the dress.

Philip smiled. "The roses must have worked, since you're dressed and ready."

Joanne sniffed. "She's allergic to roses."

"Oh. I'd forgotten."

Of course he had. Perhaps that had been the trouble. He'd considered her more of an accessory than an individual.

Joanne began to close the door, then stopped. "Well, hello," she said slowly, her voice dropping an octave. "How can I help *you*?"

"I'm looking for Charlie Nelson," came a man's voice.

Charlie looked from Philip, to Joanne gaping at the door, to the ceiling, wondering what would happen next. Somehow, the voice seemed familiar. She took a step past the leering Philip, closer to the door.

"Come right in," answered Joanne.

And Charlie knew exactly what was going to happen next: she was going to expire right on the spot, because it was none other than the Rhinestone Cowboy. How on earth had he found out where she lived? Just as she was about to ask exactly that question, Philip grabbed her arm.

"What's going on around here? Who is that man?"

Davis overheard Philip's question. He grinned and took Charlie's other arm. "I'm her date."

"I think you're mistaken. Isn't he, Charlie?" He smiled victoriously at Davis. "*I'm* her date."

Charlie understood how a tender morsel felt when being chewed over by two dogs. The room was choking with male hormones. "Philip, I told you this morning that I'm not going out with you any more."

"What about the roses?"

Charlie shook off the hands of both men, then dashed down the hall to Joanne's room. She grabbed the bucket of roses and returned to the living room and pushed the pail into Philip's arms. "Here."

"I don't get it."

"I'm allergic to them."

Joanne, still standing at the open door, laughed her head off. "There aren't any others coming, are there? And you said you'd planned a quiet night in front of the TV."

"Very funny," said Charlie as Joanne shut the door.

"I wouldn't have missed this for anything." She

crossed the foyer and joined Philip, glaring at the flowers. Davis looked smugly arrogant.

"Do you have another bucket for these?" Davis asked as he held out a dozen daisies. How had he known they were her favorite flowers?

"I'll take care of them," assured Joanne.

"Grab your shoes and let's go, Charlie," said Davis. "I don't want to wait around for more competition to arrive."

Joanne shoved the shoe box into his hands.

Charlie fought for control. Had she been plopped into some stage farce and not been given her lines? She couldn't get a word in edgewise.

Philip pulled a ring box from his pocket. "I thought we had something special, Charlie. I know I waited a long time before declaring myself, but when you broke our date, I knew the time was right."

As he started to go down on the proverbial bended knee, Charlie grabbed Davis by the arm. "Get me out of here."

"You got it, babe." He stuck the shoe box into Charlie's arms; then, like a caveman, he swept her up into his arms and carried her to the door. Joanne ran ahead and opened it. Davis grinned as he left the apartment.

Philip ran behind them. "I think I deserve an answer, Charlie!"

Davis turned back. "I just took her over the threshold, old man. Personally, I'd take that as a sign if I were you." Then he crossed the small lawn to the parking lot and tossed Charlie into his convertible Mustang. Thankfully, the top was down.

Charlie couldn't believe what was happening to her. It had to be the dress. It had to be.

Joanne came running out to the car and waved good-bye. "When I told you to take some risks, kiddo, you took me seriously! Have a great time!"

Davis grinned to himself. Things couldn't have worked out better if he'd planned. He had the girl, and she was a knockout. The only catch was that before they arrived at the country club, he had to convince her to be his fiancée for a night.

He shrugged. Piece of cake.

If only she'd stop muttering about having planned to take small steps, and let him get a word in edgewise. When it seemed she'd calmed down a bit, he spoke up. "I really appreciate your doing this, Charlie. If you ever need a fiancé, be assured, I'll be there for you, too."

"What?" She looked over at him as if she'd just become aware of where she was. "You don't expect me to go through with that fiancée business, do you?"

"Well, yeah. I sort of thought that was the game plan."

"Oh, sheesh." She rolled her eyes and leaned back in her seat. "I might have known I couldn't have a quiet night just to myself. I wanted to shampoo my hair."

"We could stop at my house on the way." Davis couldn't help teasing her. When she got miffed, that darn dimple peeped out and he had a hankering to see it again. "A scalp massage might be a great way to start our engagement."

Charlie crossed her arms over her chest and tossed her head. "Don't go getting any ideas."

"I can't help it. You look gorgeous in that dress." And she did. He shouldn't have teased her, because it made him imagine kissing the hollow at the base of her throat.

He swerved to avoid a car. He had to get his mind back onto driving and off such bachelorhood-threatening thoughts. Charlie wasn't the kind of woman a man daydreamed about unless his intentions included wedding chapels.

And the only wedding he planned to attend was his mother's.

Who'd have believed a librarian could get to him this way? "We're almost there, Cinderella. Better put your shoes on."

"They're not mine. They're Joanne's." Charlie

dove into the shoe box, then leaned down to put the shoes on. "These stilettos will be the death of me. I'll probably be crippled for life."

Davis glanced her way. There was such an endearing quality about her. He took a deep, steadying breath, finding it nearly impossible to pull his gaze away. He forced himself to look down at her shoes.

"Far be it from me to complain, Davis, but shouldn't you be watching the road instead of mentally unbuckling my shoes?"

"I have everything under control." Davis turned back to the road, a little embarrassed by being caught staring. "I was checking to see if you needed help."

Charlie snorted, a most unladylike sound.

Davis drove on in silence for a moment; then temptation got the best of him. He chanced another look at her, then gulped, thoroughly distracted. A crunch sounded, and the accompanying jar drew his attention to the mailbox he'd just crashed into.

Chapter Three

Charlie watched Davis carefully fold and refold the warning citation, then place it neatly into his wallet. Thankfully, his car hadn't suffered much damage, which couldn't be said for the mailbox he'd hit. Bricks lay tumbled all over the sidewalk.

As the police car drove off, the officer giving her a little wave, Charlie couldn't hold back her laughter any longer.

"I don't know what you find funny about the situation," groused Davis.

"Well, you did get off with a warning."

"Yeah, and a receipt for two hundred dollars in mailbox repairs." Davis slammed his wallet into the glove box with a loud snap. "This is all your fault, you know."

"My fault?"

"Yeah, you heard what the officer said."

"He's someone I know from the library. Of *course* he'd say that." Charlie felt color creeping into her face again. The whole time Lt. Brown was lecturing them about driving more carefully, she'd been unable to keep from blushing.

"Oh yeah? That you're dangerous in that outfit and creating a public nuisance?" Davis shook his head and grinned. "Got to admit he had a point—librarians like you should not be allowed out dressed like that."

"Just take me home, then."

Davis shook his head. "Not on your life. This whole evening has cost me a fortune. At the least, I'm going to get what I need out of it. You're going to meet my mother, no matter how many mailboxes I have to knock down in order to get there."

"Okay, but I draw the line at pedestrians." Charlie had to hand it to Davis, he was taking this all pretty well. "And I want to leave early."

"No more than I do." Davis shifted the car into reverse and backed out onto the street. He shot a glance at her through the corner of his eye. "Just pull down your skirt, will you?"

"Aye, Captain." Charlie tugged the skirt as low as she could, which wasn't much. She shifted and tucked her legs as far under the seat as possible. Then she giggled. "It's nice that you like my legs."

Davis growled, put the car in forward and shot down the street.

"I think we should talk," mused Charlie. She needed to know a lot more about Davis before meeting his mother. Like his birthday, for starters. And his mother's name might be a bonus.

"What do we need to talk about? If you're going to harass me about my driving, forget it. Until now, I've never even been in a fender bender."

"You said that your mom won't marry the man she loves until you're settled. Why don't you just get married?"

"Women are all alike, aren't they? The first thing they want to know is why any single man chooses to stay that way—single. I'm enjoying myself. I'm having the time of my life." Davis carefully turned a corner. Despite having run off the road, he appeared to be a very careful driver.

"Besides," added Davis, "I haven't had time for romance. I've been too busy making a living. And now, just when I get a chance to do what I've always wanted, buy my ranch, this comes up. Mom wants to marry Jim Turner and won't because she doesn't want me to be lonely. They'll be moving to Tokyo."

"I should at least know your mother's name."

"Ellen Murphy."

"Is there anything I should know about her?"

Charlie felt as though she were groping around in the dark and Davis was blowing out the matches.

"She's my mother. What's to know?"

"So tell me about yourself. I should know *something* about you if we're engaged."

Davis turned down the drive leading into the country club, then pulled up to the valet parking attendant. Davis handed over his keys to the attendant, then rushed around the car to help Charlie out. Opening her door, he reached in and took her hand.

She liked the feel of his hand, firm but not rough. Gentle without being soft.

"You don't need to worry," said Davis. "I've got it all figured out."

"You do?"

"Yeah. It was love at first sight. The moment we laid eyes on each other, we knew it was destiny."

Destined to become fast enemies is more like it, thought Charlie.

Davis shot her a reproving look. Her cynical expression must have given her away. She schooled her face to show no emotion.

"Mom'll eat it up," he insisted. He placed his hand on Charlie's back as he led her into the building.

Charlie shivered, and sped up her pace, feeling threatened by the possessiveness of his touch.

Davis didn't take the hint. He merely increased

his own step to match hers, leaving her feeling breathless when she needed to be logical. "I don't know anything about you other than your propensity to knock down mailboxes. Won't your mom notice?"

He grinned. "We haven't known each other long. We just know it's right between us."

"Oh, that's good." She had to admire his approach, since it would cover any awkward lacks of knowledge that one would generally expect in an engaged couple. How could his mother argue against love at first sight? Rather than guessing the engagement was a ruse, she'd be worrying about Davis acting impetuously. He was more cunning than she'd given him credit for, and after the way he'd spirited her out of her apartment, that was saying a lot.

She fought to keep her jaw from dropping when they entered the large country club ballroom. The main color theme—scarlet red—was in the exact shade as her dress. Valentine hearts of various shapes cascaded from strings tied to the ceiling along with pink, red, and maroon balloons. Round tables, dressed in what appeared to be white Brandenburg lace over scarlet linen, created a doily effect. A string ensemble, clad in tuxedos with scarlet cummerbunds, discreetly played classical music in one corner of the chandeliered ballroom.

"What is this?" asked Charlie as she gazed at the cupid cutouts placed strategically on the walls. "The Rocky Horror Country Club?"

"Think of it as lifestyles of the cheap and tasteless." Davis pointed at the mirrored ball reflecting red lights as it twirled over the dance floor. "Better hurry, it's the flashing red light special."

"I'd love to meet the decorator," replied Charlie, relieved that Davis hadn't been offended by her reaction.

"Rodney Dangerfield's dresser?"

Charlie grinned up at him. "No, I'm sure it was done by Weird Al Yankovich. Are you sure your mother is here?"

"Yeah, she joined during her Howard Stern listening period." He gazed around the room. "I think that's Jim and her under the plastic mistletoe in the corner."

Davis took Charlie's hand. "Feeling nervous?"

Butterflies danced in a frenzy in the pit of her stomach, if that could be called nerves. How had she gone from wanting to play it a little less safe to pretending to be engaged to a man she didn't even know? She took a deep breath. "A little, but it might be because the décor is so overdone."

Davis gave her an encouraging smile, then pulled her toward the mistletoe.

"Is that your mom waving to us?"

Davis nodded. "Time to enter the lion's den."

"She looks sweet."

"Oh, she's a great sport. I'm certain you'll like each other." Hadn't that been the main reason he'd been determined to convince Charlie to be his fiancée?

"I can understand now why you needed me," she commented as they wove between tables.

"Because you and Mom will hit it off?"

"No. If this place is similar to your taste in women, I'd be leery of bringing 'em home to mama, too."

Davis bit back a retort as they reached the plastic mistletoe. He wiped the annoyed expression off his face and traded it for a big toothy smile, which was the best he could do to cover his frustration. "Hi Mom, Jim."

After exchanging the customary hug and handshake, Davis introduced Charlie, who'd wiped the naughty smile from her face and was doing her best to act like the perfect fiancée. He just hoped they weren't overdoing it. As he helped her into the chair, he said, "Let me help you, dear."

"Why, thanks so much, darling." She batted her eyelashes at him, then turned to give a huge smile to Ellen and Jim.

"I live to do things for you, precious," he said, wanting to even things up a little. That's when

Charlie stabbed his foot with her stiletto heel. It *had* been a bit much, but it was her fault—he'd forgotten what they were trying to accomplish with the way she kept trying to one-up him. Trying not to limp, he took his own seat.

Ellen and Jim watched them both as if they were trying not to laugh. So much for their first impression. Davis couldn't think of a thing to say, and Charlie just sat there with a vapid smile.

Finally, Jim jumped into the silence. "I can see now why Davis was in such a hurry to catch up with you yesterday, Charlie. You're prettier up close than you are from a distance, and that's saying a lot."

Charlie colored slightly. "Thank you. I'm pleased to finally meet you both. Davis has told me so much about you."

Davis was impressed with the way she appeared so composed. She shot him a look from under her lashes, which he took to mean she knew what she was doing. He breathed a sigh of relief.

Charlie said, "Davis mentioned that you'll soon be going to Tokyo, Jim."

Jim nodded, his jaw tightening, reminding Davis of what he wanted to accomplish.

Davis cleared his throat. "We need some champagne. I have some news you've been waiting a long time to hear, Mom."

His mother captured his eyes with her own. They were so much like his, deep brown. Ellen's had more crinkles at the corners, and a warm loving light seemed to pour out from them whenever she looked directly at him.

Davis placed his arm around Charlie's shoulders and drew closer. "Mom, Jim, Charlie has agreed to become my wife."

He held his breath, waiting for their reaction.

"What? How wonderful!" Ellen reached across the table to take one of Charlie's hands. "I'm so thrilled to welcome you to our family, dear."

Davis released Charlie and his breath. His mother did seem pleased. That was step one. The next would be to get Jim to pop the question again. Right now, he looked uncomfortable, as if he planned to blow everything. Davis had to find a way to prevent that from happening.

His mother asked, "Have you set the date yet?"

Charlie said, "No," just as Davis said, "Sometime in the fall."

They both laughed nervously. Davis added, "Well, you can see I've got my work cut out for me getting her to the altar." He reached forward and took her hand, then pulled it to his lips. "I'm just glad she'll have me at all."

"Well, I'd love to hear all the details," Ellen said.

Charlie cast him a look not unlike a frightened

colt. She pulled back her hands and stood. "If you'll excuse me, I need to powder my nose."

Ellen asked, "Do you want me to show you the way?"

"Oh no," Charlie quickly reassured her. "You'll have a lot to talk about with Davis. I'll only be a few minutes."

Leaning down and kissing his cheek, she said, "Parting is such sweet sorrow. Try not to miss me too much, dear."

Davis hissed, "Chicken."

She patted him on the head and shot him a wide grin as she walked away. Davis turned back to face his mother.

"She seems perfect for you, Davis."

"So, you like her?"

"I don't really know her yet, but I'm sure with time we'll become the best of friends." She grinned at Jim, then looked back at Davis. "It's obvious you belong together, and I couldn't be more delighted that you've finally found that right someone."

Jim looked a bit less upset. Instead, he wore a grin that didn't bode well. "I agree. You suit each other, and if I'd picked a woman for you I couldn't have done better. I hope you know how lucky you are."

"Davis, why don't you run to the bar and get us

some punch?" asked his mother. "I want to toast your happiness."

Reluctantly, he pushed back his chair, giving Jim a warning look. Jim winked, then said, "I think they've got punch in a fountain on the buffet."

Davis didn't have much choice other than to obey their implied order to scram, as much as he wanted to stay and make sure Jim wouldn't give the game away. Mom was going to have her chance at love, and celebrating her nuptials was something he very much intended to do before too long.

Charlie waited ten minutes before leaving the ladies room, hoping that would give Davis time to answer Ellen's questions. She was certain Ellen would want to know all the details, and Charlie wasn't ready to provide any, especially since she didn't know them herself.

She left the ladies room and made her way back to the table. As she got closer, she wondered where Davis had gone. Ellen and Jim were in quiet conversation. Charlie felt reluctant to join them just yet. Hanging back a bit, she heard Davis's mom say, "I know it's in here."

Jim laughed as Ellen patted his jacket pocket. "You know me too well."

"That's one of the things I love best about you." She reached into his jacket and pulled out what appeared to be a ring box from his inner pocket. Pushing it into Jim's hand, she looked into his eyes and said, "Ask me again."

Jim gulped.

"You don't think you're going to run off to Tokyo without me, do you? I'm certain your head would be turned by all those women in kimonos and you'd quickly forget me. I can't take that risk." Ellen leaned forward and gave him a quick kiss. "Ask me, Jim."

Jim looked as if he was afraid to say anything for fear the spell might break.

"If you don't do it, you'll force me to ask you, and I'd really rather not. It would set a bad precedent." She ran her hand down the side of his face. "Please, Jim?"

Jim whispered something, but Charlie didn't catch the words, although she knew the meaning. She saw Ellen nod, tears of joy spilling from her eyes, and Charlie felt her eyes well up, too.

She hated eavesdropping, but in some way was glad she'd done so. Davis had been right—the issue of him being settled was what had prevented Ellen from making a commitment to Jim. Down deep inside, Charlie longed to find the love and contentment that Davis's mother had with Jim.

The fiancée façade had reminded her how very empty she felt. Well, something good was coming from her deception—she was learning how to take risks, which would possibly lead to an end to her inner loneliness. It had to.

Jim was holding Ellen's face in his big brown hands, murmuring words of love. On her finger twinkled a diamond.

Just then, Charlie sensed Davis nearby. Turning, she saw him heading toward her with a crystal cup in each hand. When he reached her, she nodded toward the couple at the table. "Your plan worked, Davis. Look at them."

Charlie watched Davis as he gazed at his mother, a tension easing from his face and shoulders, as if he'd been holding himself in check. His expression softened, and Charlie wondered what it would feel like to have him look at her that way, with so much caring and love. He might be a Lothario, but he was a nice one. "Let's not disturb them."

"Okay. I've got to get more punch. Want to help?"

"Sure."

He handed her one of the cups and waited while she took a sip of the too-sweet pink punch.

She crinkled her nose at the taste. "You've got to admit that when this club does a color theme, they go all the way."

He grinned, led her toward the buffet, then nodded back toward their table. "Thanks, Charlie, for helping make my mom happy."

"Anytime. I'm thinking of starting up a new business, *Fiancée for Hire*."

"You'd be very successful. I'll give you a reference."

Charlie rolled her eyes at his patently false charm as they reached the buffet. She gazed at the overly ornate cupid fountain spewing punch from his mouth.

She turned to Davis and smiled sweetly. "He looks just like you."

Chapter Four

Davis was tempted, for a moment, to dunk Charlie into the punch bowl. Amazing how one pint-sized female could tie him in knots. If they'd been in grade school, he'd be dipping her braids into an inkwell or sticking toads down the back of her dress. As an adult, however, he didn't have those options, appealing though they might be.

Fighting an urge to tickle her until she begged him to stop, he said, "We don't resemble each other in the least."

"Look at his profile."

He made a show of stepping to the side and examining the cupid carefully, then shook his head. "Don't see it."

Charlie laughed. "Serves you right for making me

come tonight and then trying to sweet-talk me. Besides, your expression was priceless."

It probably had been. He should have realized that the dimple playing mischievously about her mouth was indicative of her personality. They'd better get out of here before he did something he'd regret—like kissing her.

"Being the butt of your jokes is a small price to pay for Mom's happiness. Let's drink to their future—then we can leave."

Charlie was astonished by a momentary disappointment. She'd actually been enjoying herself with Davis. She grabbed another punch cup, then headed toward the table with Davis following close behind, carrying cups as before. When they arrived, Ellen beamed at both of them.

"Exactly on cue," said Jim as he took a cup from Charlie and handed it to Ellen, then accepted his from Davis. "We've got two engagements to toast tonight."

"Don't tell me Mom finally agreed?" Davis asked, as if he hadn't already known. Although Charlie knew his surprise wasn't genuine, his delight as he stooped to kiss his mother's cheek couldn't have been feigned. Davis helped Charlie into her seat, then turned to shake Jim's hand. "It's about time."

"I'm so pleased you're happy, Davis," said his

mother as Davis took his chair. She held up her cup, then gazed into Jim's eyes. "To the most romantic Valentine's Day ever."

As she took a sip, Charlie's heart ached at the love she saw between the couple. What amazed her was that Ellen would have sacrificed it all for Davis.

Although Charlie had some memories of her own mother, they weren't as complete as she'd like. Mom and Dad had been killed when she was eight and her brothers, Monty Joe, then eighteen, and Bobby Gray, seventeen, had stepped in to raise her. But she couldn't ever remember anyone putting her happiness before their own. Perhaps it was because she'd been an unexpected blessing, a late in life baby and then, later, as much a burden as a responsibility.

Davis was extremely fortunate, and she could understand why he'd go to such lengths to ensure his mother's happiness. She barely knew her, yet she felt protective of her, too.

"This is all happening so fast." Ellen laughed, her eyes glowing with happiness. "Jim suggested we get married next weekend at his cabin on Lake Texoma."

"I bought it with you in mind," added Jim. "That gazebo will be the perfect spot to say our vows."

"We thought we'd call Judge Hawkins to see if he can perform the ceremony." Ellen, looking closer to Davis's age than her own, smiled down at the ring resting on her finger.

"Hawkins had better do it," said Jim with a laugh, "or I'll have his scrawny hide."

Ellen playfully slapped at his hand. "Seriously, there are a ton of things we'll have to do this week—marriage license, blood tests—" A look of alarm clouded her face. "—and shopping and packing."

"Don't worry," said Davis. "You'll get it all done. If there's anything I can do to help, you know you can count on me."

"Thanks," said Jim. "We knew we could. And I do have a favor to ask."

"Name it."

"That you'll stand up with me as my best man?"

Davis didn't say anything for a moment. Charlie watched him as he froze, then swallowed, trying to check his emotions.

It was as if a façade was being stripped from him. He wasn't just a cowboy, a businessman, or an eligible bachelor. Davis had a depth she'd never have suspected if she hadn't been included in this tableau.

At last he got out the words, "I'd be honored, Jim. Deeply honored."

His eyes looked moist. Charlie lowered her head, aware that she was only here as an outsider. A slight flush of embarrassment itched at her conscience. Perhaps she should have excused herself again. Trying to tune out the conversation, she traced the lacy pattern covering the table with her forefinger, following first a swirl that she realized was actually a pineapple. The lace was more complex than she'd thought at first—like Davis.

The sound of her name called her back.

Ellen looked at her through worried eyes. "I know it's a lot to ask on such short acquaintance." She shot a glance at Jim, who took her hand. "But since we're going to be family . . ."

Davis coughed. "What Mom's trying to ask, Charlie, is if you'd be her maid of honor. It would mean a lot to her, a lot to all of us."

Ellen, Jim and Davis were silent, watching her, waiting. What could she say to get out of it? She wasn't really going to be part of this family. And did Davis really want her to be included? After all, he knew she was a phony. "I . . . I don't know what to say," she finally stuttered, a ball of misery settling deep in her chest.

"Please say you will, dear?" Ellen asked breathlessly.

Charlie watched Davis to see what he wanted her to do. "I think I'm scheduled to work next weekend."

He draped his arm around her. "I'm sure your

boss would understand if you explained the situation."

Ellen, measuring out her words, added, "If it's a problem, I suppose we could have the wedding in Dallas, at my house." She tried to look like it was a good idea, but Charlie could see that Ellen was attempting, again, to sacrifice herself for someone else's comfort.

That decided her. As much as she'd feel like an interloper and even more of a liar, she'd be there to make Ellen happy. "No. I'll trade weekends with another librarian. She owes me, anyway. I'd be delighted to be your maid of honor, Ellen."

"Oh, this is going to be perfect." A tear trickled down Ellen's happy face. She turned to Jim. "I can't believe it—it's all falling together as if it's meant to be."

"It *is* meant to be," assured Jim with a gruff voice. He pulled a handkerchief from his pocket and dabbed at Ellen's face. "Now, no more tears. It's time for a toast."

"I'll second that," said Davis. He held up his cup, "To the most deserving couple I know. May your love last an eternity and your happiness grow each day."

Ellen added, "And to my son and his bride-to-be. May you find happiness and completeness in all of life's little tribulations." She waited a second, then added, "And may there be many grandchildren for me to spoil."

"I'll drink to that," said Jim.

"Hold on a minute! Let us get hitched before demanding grandkids," Davis said with a mock look of fear on his face. "Now that I think about it, I always disliked being an only child. The two of you need to get to work producing a half-brother for me."

"My child-bearing years are long past," said Ellen with a sassy gleam in her eyes. "Charlie and you are now in charge of infant production."

Charlie laughed. A true daughter-to-be couldn't have fallen in love with Ellen any faster than Charlie had tonight. Ellen was terrific, and even Davis didn't appreciate her as he should. If he did, he'd have brought a real fiancée home to meet his mother long before now.

"We could make this a double wedding," suggested Ellen.

The arm Davis had draped nonchalantly over Charlie's shoulders tightened. She quickly answered, "We haven't known each other that long, Ellen. We've discussed it and feel it would be best if we learn more about each other first."

"You see what I'm having to deal with?" Davis threw up his hands. "I'm lucky to have gotten this far with her."

"It's your own fault. If you hadn't had a string of women before me, maybe I wouldn't worry so much." She narrowed her eyes at him in jest. "I wouldn't want you to grow bored."

"That could never happen," Davis shot back.

He released her, then traced his forefinger down the bridge of her nose, sending warmth to the length of her nerve endings. He was awfully good at this couple-in-love stuff, she thought, trying to keep in mind it was all pretend.

"I can't think of anyone more stimulating than you," he said. "Guess I don't have any choice but to get you to the altar as fast as can be, before some other guy tries to stake a claim."

Charlie tossed her head, more to get away from her reaction to his touch than because she was thrown by his words. She shrugged. "What girl could say no to a guy who begs so nicely?"

"It was worth a try," said Ellen. "But you have to let me know as soon as you set the date. I'd like to come and help out in the plans, if I may?"

"I'd love your help. Thank you." She would have meant it, too, if there really was going to be a wedding. Which there wasn't. But it would be lovely to have a future mother like Ellen to help plan one.

"I imagine your own mother, though, will be very involved."

Charlie shook her head. "I'm an orphan, so having your advice would mean a lot."

Davis shot her a surprised look, then nodded at his mother. "We'll call you as soon as Charlie makes her mind up about the date."

"I'll be waiting. If you'd like, Charlie, why don't you and Davis come up to the lake Friday evening? Maybe we could look through a few bride magazines and get to know each other better?"

"That sounds great." Davis looked pleased. "I'd love to teach you to fish, Charlie."

"Oh, you would?" She batted her lashes at him and his assumption she wouldn't know anything about the sport. Her brothers had always made her bait their hooks. She was very good at fishing, and savored the idea of teaching him a thing or two about making assumptions. "That sounds great, Ellen. I wouldn't miss it."

Ellen grinned and Charlie sensed it was because she knew exactly what Charlie had been thinking.

Jim handed Ellen her handbag and scarf, saying, "We've got a lot to do before next weekend." He winked at Ellen, who blushed.

"Oh, right. A lot to do." Taking his extended hand, she stood. "I hate to toast and run—"

Jim cut her off by kissing her forehead. "You don't."

Ellen laughed. "He's right. I don't hate to toast

and run, but we did promise you dinner. You will feel free to stay and have whatever you like, won't you? I am genuinely delighted to have met you, Charlie, and look forward to next weekend."

"Don't worry about us," said Davis.

With that, Jim pulled her away, saying, "We'll be in touch."

"I adore your mother, Davis." Charlie sighed and leaned back in her chair, allowing herself to relax.

"I knew you two would hit it off."

"You were right." Running back over events, she agreed that things had gone very well, when suddenly she realized that she'd just agreed to another weekend of playacting. "Are you sure you want me to be there next weekend, Davis? It's not too late to think up some excuse."

"I need you there. Mom might go through with the wedding, but she'd worry that there was a problem between us."

"That's what I'd decided. This fiancée business is a lot more difficult than I thought it would be." And volunteering to prolong it was probably the stupidest thing she'd ever done.

"Yeah. You ready to go?"

"And leave this place of beauty and elegance?" Charlie smiled. "I can't wait. I keep feeling like all those cupids are looking at me with accusing eyes."

Davis grinned. "I think they're looking at you in a slightly different way." His gaze met hers.

He's forgotten to stop acting, she told herself, trying not to drown in the depths of his eyes. She hopped from her chair. "Let's go."

"Don't you think that orphan business was over-doing it?"

"I *am* an orphan."

"I thought you'd said it to get out of having to introduce your parents." In fact, he'd been sure of it. He'd only brought it up because she'd been so nervous when he'd referred to how good she looked.

He wondered if she was unaware of how attractive she was. Maybe she was impervious to him, really didn't find him attractive or even likeable. He didn't like that idea one bit.

She had such unusual charm—one moment sweet and innocent, and the next saying something completely unexpected and outrageous. When she turned that smile on him, it took every bit of will-power he could muster to keep things between them strictly business.

As they left the ballroom and walked down the hallway to the exit, he wondered what had stopped him from kissing her. Maybe the confusion in her eyes? Maybe the need for some reassurance?

"You said you liked my mom."

She nodded.

"Do you like me, too? Even a little?"

Her eyes widened. His question surprised him as much as it surprised her.

Then her dimple peeped out. "You've grown on me—sort of like fungus."

"I can live with that." He pulled her to him.

"What are you doing?"

"Shut up."

"Davis!"

"I'm kissing you, silly. Close your eyes." Her lips formed an "o" as he lowered his to meet them.

She tasted like orange spice.

Then he heard his mother's voice. "Maybe we'd better make it a double wedding after all, if you two can't behave better than this in public."

Davis stepped back from Charlie, with a feeling similar to the times his mother had caught him with his hand in the cookie jar. When had he ever acted like this before? His mom was right—he wasn't some overly hormoned teenager, and it was time to stop acting like one.

He glanced at Charlie. Her eyes were still half-closed. She opened her eyes slowly, and as she saw his mother, color gradually climbed her neck and face. Then she yanked Davis by the lapels, drawing him down so she could whisper, "I don't know how yet, but I'm going to get even with you for this."

She released him and turned to his mother and smiled sweetly. "You may have a point. Good night."

"Come along, Davis," she continued, glancing back at him. She grabbed him by the necktie and practically dragged him out of the building and into the parking lot.

"You can let go now."

She did, sending him out of balance. She kept walking at a steady pace.

Davis hurried to catch up. Something was obviously eating at her. "What's wrong?"

She stopped and turned to face him. "Let's get one thing clear here. I'm not one of your women, Davis. I'm a free agent who's simply trying to help out. You got that?"

"I never said you were."

"Well, that kiss back there said something else."

It had only been a brief little kiss, even if it had knocked him on his solar plexus. But she was overlooking one detail. "You kissed me back."

"I'm not sure I did."

He grinned.

"Even if I did kiss you, it must have been because of all that punch," she gritted out, then started her march again, until she reached his car. She crossed her arms and waited for him to open the door.

Davis felt a surge of confidence. It hadn't been

the non-alcoholic punch. Deny it all she wanted to, but she liked him.

He unlocked her door, noticing that she stepped out of arm distance while he did so. "You're right. You aren't like other women. Truce?"

She visibly relented, her arms dropping to her sides as she got in the passenger seat. "I'll think about it."

When they reached her apartment, Charlie tried to get Davis to stay in the car, but he refused, insisting he escort her back. Not knowing what she could say to discourage him, she shrugged, then marched ahead as if they weren't together. Upon arriving at her door, she offered her hand. "Good night."

Rather than shaking hands, Davis stuck the shoe box into her outstretched palm, then reached up to tuck a strand of her hair behind her ear. "Thanks again for everything."

She stiffened when he paused, and wondered if he was going to try to kiss her again. Instead, though, he leaned close and kissed her forehead, then walked away.

She watched him sashay to his car, evidently pleased with himself, and she wanted to do something to even the score. At least he wouldn't have the last word. "Don't forget to buy me a ring."

That stopped him. He turned to face her. "Thanks. I'd forgotten that."

Not exactly the reaction she'd hoped for, but it was a start.

He shot her a chagrined smile. "Do you know your ring size?"

"Six."

He nodded, then turned and walked a few paces back toward her. "Are you sure you don't want to pick it out yourself? I'm not good at this kind of thing."

"There's no way I'm going to go buy my own engagement ring, even if it is a bogus engagement." She wasn't going to let him off the hook. "This is something you'll have to do on your own."

"But aren't there different types and styles?" he wheedled, trying to make himself sound dumb and male.

On the other hand, all the indications showed he *was* a dumb male. If he wasn't, he wouldn't want to be a cowboy.

"I don't even know if you want yellow or white gold."

"I'm sure you'll have no problem, Davis." She stepped into her apartment. Then she smiled. As she closed the door, she added, "Just buy one with a diamond to match your ego—extra-large."

Chapter Five

At the sound of Davis's laughter, Charlie bolted her apartment door. She headed to the kitchen, as she always did when she was upset.

The man was too good at this couple business, and she didn't like feeling out of control.

She kicked off the killer shoes and swung open the refrigerator. Time for more chocolate pie.

When Joanne returned from her date, Charlie was sitting at the bar with an empty plate in front of her.

"You didn't eat the whole thing, did you?"

Charlie patted her abdomen. "I may have to buy all new clothes after this binge."

Joanne grabbed a glass of milk. "You didn't have fun with Davis?"

"Hardly. He's the most pig-headed, arrogant man

I've ever met." She wasn't going to let herself think about the moments when he'd actually been fun to be around.

"Sounds like most men. What did he do to set you off?"

"He kissed me," Charlie said, accusingly.

Joanne laughed. "What's so bad about that?"

"His mother saw us."

"I bet that was uncomfortable."

Charlie buried her face in her hands. "He's a cowboy, or the next thing to it. How could I kiss him?"

"I thought he kissed you."

"I might have kissed him back."

"Aren't you sure?"

Charlie moaned. "It must have been a reflex action."

Joanne handed her a glass of water and two aspirin. "Wash 'em down, sweetie, and look on the bright side."

Charlie took the aspirin. "What bright side?"

"You don't ever have to see him again."

"That's what you think. His plans worked *too* well. We're spending the weekend together."

"What?!" Joanne looked at her as if she'd gone off the deep end. "When I said to loosen up a little, I didn't mean—"

"It's far worse than that. His mother is getting married next weekend."

"That's great."

"Yeah, great. Fantastic even." Bubbles of hysteria rose in her chest. "*I'm* going to be her maid of honor."

"You mean you're going to be his fiancée for an entire *weekend*? I hope you know what you're doing."

"I haven't a clue." What was it about the Murphys that could influence her to do things she had no intention of doing? "I think I'll bake another pie."

The entire week had been quiet, almost too quiet. Everything had been silent on the Murphy front. There was nothing this Thursday morning that indicated it would be any different.

Sitting at her desk in the library, Charlie reached over and picked up the jingling phone receiver. "Research, Charlie Nelson speaking. How may I help you?"

She'd said the same spiel so often, she did it at home by accident and suspected she did it in her sleep, too. This time, however, it wasn't a library customer calling.

"Charlie? This is Ellen Murphy, dear."

"Ellen?" Charlie hadn't expected Davis's mother

to call. If anything, things had been so calm at home and work this week, she was sort of hoping she'd been forgotten. No such luck.

"How are you doing, dear?"

Charlie jammed her pencil into the silver pencil cup on her desk, accidently tumbling the contents. "Just fine. And you?"

"It's been a marvelous week, frantic but lovely. I'm calling for a couple of reasons. First is to discuss the wedding. We never talked about what you should wear, and I thought you'd feel more comfortable if we discussed it."

"Oh, that totally slipped my mind," said Charlie as she grabbed at the writing implements rolling from her desk. She bent to retrieve a couple of pens. "I'm so glad you called."

Her forgetfulness showed how in denial she was about this weekend. She hadn't even considered what to pack. If Ellen hadn't called, Charlie might have spent the next afternoon in a panic when she realized she didn't know what to wear. "Do I need to buy a dress?"

"I feel guilty for not calling you sooner. The wedding is going to be informal. I'm going to wear a suit, so hopefully you already own something that will work?"

"I've got a couple of dresses or a suit that might work." She tried to visualize wearing her navy suit.

Too conservative for a wedding. She'd look like she was attending a funeral. Maybe one of her dresses. "Do you have a color preference?"

"I think you'd look lovely in blue, but any color will do. I saw a couple of dresses at Rose's Dress Shop at the mall which might do if you need to buy something. The prices were very reasonable. But, honestly, dear, any color will be fine. Have you given any thought to your colors?"

"My colors?" For a moment, she couldn't think what Ellen meant. Charlie's brain finally kicked in. "Oh, you mean for my wedding? Davis and I haven't talked about details yet."

"Oh, well." Ellen sounded disappointed, then her tone became cheerful. "I'm sure you have plenty of time to decide on all those pesky details. I'm so looking forward to getting to know you better, which brings me to the other reason I called. What time do you generally finish up at work?"

"I get off at five." Charlie spotted some loose change that had spilled from the cup as well as several paperclips. She threw them in her desk drawer.

"Perfect!"

Charlie realized she should have asked why before answering. She stopped herself from screaming, *What now?*

"A few of my friends are putting together an impromptu bridal shower for me today at five-thirty."

She laughed. "They thought the perfect place for a send-off is Murphy Title's conference room, so that's where it'll be held. Do you think you can make it?"

Charlie tried desperately to think up some excuse for not going, but her brain seemed to be malfunctioning.

"I'm looking forward to introducing my future daughter-in-law to my friends. You can make it, can't you?"

Charlie's stomach sank. How many people were going to become embroiled due to Davis's little scheme? Sooner or later, this was all going to come back to haunt her, and she suspected it would be sooner, not later. "I may have a conflict but I'll do my best to come."

"Thanks so much, dear. I'll let you get back to work. Do try to come. I'd love to have the chance to chat."

"I'll do my best. Thanks so much for calling. I'm ashamed that I hadn't thought to ask you about what to wear." Charlie found another pen and placed it in the cup, then wiped off her desk.

"Don't worry. Davis is like his father. When we were engaged, I didn't know whether I was coming or going." Ellen laughed, "I'm sure Davis has you as confused as I was."

"I'm relieved you understand."

"Oh, I do. And here's a tidbit to relieve your mind." Ellen paused. "At least it was in my mind during Davis's father's courtship. Murphy men play the field before marriage, but once they make a choice, they take it seriously—they mate for life."

"That's reassuring." She wondered if Murphy wives were known for their rose-colored glasses. She couldn't imagine Davis ever deliberately choosing to settle down. "Thanks for telling me."

"Good. See you later, I hope."

After hanging up the phone, Charlie placed her head in her hands. She'd been doing that a lot lately. Rubbing her temples, she fought off a threatening headache. She didn't have time for it. Somehow, she had to figure out what to wear to the wedding, and if she didn't have anything suitable, she'd have to buy something.

And then there was the shower. She had to make up her mind.

The phone rang again. "Research, Charlie Nelson. How may I help you?"

"Hi, this is Lily del Rietz, president of Murphy Title."

"How can I help you?"

"We're throwing an impromptu wedding shower for Ellen Murphy today at Murphy Title and I called to invite you. It's at five-thirty."

"Yes, Ellen called, too."

"Oh great, you're coming then. We're all dying to meet the woman who finally lassoed Davis's heart." Lily chortled. "You should have seen him mooning around here until you agreed to marry him. Kept referring to you as an elf."

Charlie held back a laugh. *Elf* was probably his substitute word for something not quite so polite. "I can't make any promises, but I'll do my best to be there."

"Thanks. I'm looking forward to meeting you."

The headache Charlie had been fighting came roaring to life as she hung up the receiver. Immediately, the phone rang again. She cautiously lifted it. "Research, Charlie Nelson—"

"Charlie! This is Jim."

"Oh, hi." Not another of Davis's cohorts. "If you're calling about the shower—"

"I see someone else beat me to the punch. Are you coming?"

"I'm not sure if I'll be able to—"

"I sure wish you would. Davis told me all about his scheme. I'd sure appreciate it if you went tonight. It would make Ellen mighty happy."

"It wouldn't be wrong to go?" She pulled a pencil from the cup and twiddled it in her fingers.

"Staying away would be worse. Now, don't forget to get the ring from Davis first."

"Shoot—I'd forgotten all about the ring."

"Ellen will want you to show it off to all her friends."

The pencil snapped. Looking down, she saw she'd broken it cleanly in half. "I'll give Davis a call and see what he wants me to do."

"You do that, hon. Now I've got an appointment, so I'd better let you go."

"Thanks for calling."

As she hung up, Charlie asked herself how all this had started. She'd wanted to take a few little risks. Baby-step risks. Little things. But what had it gained her? A whole community of people to deceive.

The red dress. That crimson man-trap must be cursed. All she'd done was buy one little red dress. Who would suspect it could cause all these problems?

She should have known there was no such thing as small risks. They only came in one size, extra-large catastrophe.

The phone jingled again. Charlie hesitated before answering it. "Research. Charlie Nelson."

"Hi, Charlie, we need to talk."

Philip's voice grated down her spine. Who else was going to call today? She never received personal calls at work, or at least so rarely she could count all the calls from the past month on one finger. "What's up?"

"I've done some thinking, and I believe you're wrong about not seeing each other. I was serious when I proposed."

She couldn't help but suspect the only reason he'd even thought of marrying her was because she'd dumped him before he had the chance to think of it first. What was it about the forbidden that seemed to appeal to men? "We don't have anything in common. I think that says it all."

"Meet me for dinner tonight and let's talk."

"I already have plans." Plans to either attend a shower or hide under her bed.

"You're going out with that Neanderthal again, aren't you?"

"No, Philip." Not only hadn't he been the one to break up with her—now he was jealous because another man seemed interested.

She thought of all the lonely nights she'd spent over the years. If only she'd realized that the secret to getting men's attention was making them believe they had competition. And if that was true, surely the reverse would be as well. "That was just a joke. He's not seriously interested in me. I'm going to a bridal shower tonight. Now, if you don't mind, I need to get back to work."

"And you're sure you don't want to reconsider my proposal?" He sounded a lot less certain of himself. So much for being serious and wanting to talk.

"No. I have to run now. Bye." Biting back a laugh, Charlie replaced the receiver. What was happening to her?

The phone chirped again. She snatched up her handbag and literally ran from her desk. No telling who was calling now and what they'd want from her. She might have known the peace couldn't last.

As she headed toward her car, she saw Jane behind the checkout desk. "I'm going to lunch."

"But it's only ten forty-five!"

Not even eleven o'clock? She checked her watch. *Sheesh. It felt like the end of the day.* "I'm starving. I'll be back." Rushing out the door, she made a beeline for her car.

She simply had to get away from the phone. Tossing her bag into the passenger seat, she started the engine. But where should she go? Charlie steered her car in the direction of the mall and Rose's Dress Shop.

It probably wasn't a bad idea to look at some dresses. Every time she'd opened her closet this week, all her outfits seemed dull and drab. She could use something more colorful—though she would steer clear of any shade of red.

On Thursday morning, Davis picked Jim up on the way to the mall, glad for the company. He'd put off buying a ring for Charlie for as long as his conscience would let him. But they were supposed to go to the lake on Friday and he didn't have much time left.

There was just something about buying an engagement ring that made it seem real, rather than the masquerade it really was. At least the mall would have window displays and lots of choices.

The parking lot wasn't as crowded mid-week as it was on weekends, making parking easy. Entering the mall through a side entrance, Davis saw they were almost alone in the spoke of shops leading from the main mall area. The sound of their footsteps seemed to echo off the glass windows.

As they neared the store directory, Jim spoke up. "I'm glad you're buying Charlie a ring."

"Well, if I didn't, Mom would suspect that something was wrong."

"Are you telling me you still aren't serious about Charlie? I've always wondered what drove you to date so many women, but wrote it off to your not having met the right girl." He shrugged. "I never thought I'd have a fool for a stepson."

Davis didn't like being called a fool, even by Jim. He glanced around, thankful no one was in earshot. "What is this? You knew from the beginning the whole engagement thing was strictly for Mom's sake."

"Anyone who's met Charlie knows what a gem

she is and how exactly right she is for you. I expected you to be smart enough to see that."

"I don't want to argue with you, Jim, but I'm having the time of my life right now. Why would I want to get hitched, other than to make sure Mom marries you?"

"Have you considered the fact that you're surrounded by people but you're going to be terribly alone once your mom and I head out to Tokyo? Your life is empty, Davis, and once you get that ranch you've been working toward, it's not going to mean a hill of beans without someone to share it. Cows make lousy company, and you won't even have Murphy Title to keep you occupied."

Davis didn't bother considering whether Jim was right or not. He clenched his jaw, determined to keep his temper in check. He hadn't given Jim any reason to think he was more serious about Charlie than any other woman. He'd been totally up-front about his motivations for even bringing her into their lives. If it weren't for needing a fiancée, he'd never have considered dating her. Jim was dead wrong. "I have plenty of female company."

"That's not what I mean and you know it." Jim reached the store directory and turned to face Davis. "I hate to give you lectures as if I were your father, but I've always felt as though you were the son I never had. Even if that wasn't the case, I owe it to you as a friend."

Davis shifted uncomfortably. He opened his mouth to speak but Jim interrupted him.

"Before I drop the subject, I have to ask—aren't you denying this a little too much?"

Davis sighed, his gaze focusing on the large clock in the main mall, rather than on his friend.

Jim continued, "You're so stubborn about living the bachelor's life, you can't admit there are fantastic advantages to giving it up. Believe me, I know. What I have with your mother couldn't compare to dates with a thousand women. When you learn that lesson, I just hope it won't be too late. Now, let's go find that jewelry store."

"I'll think about it, Jim. I've always valued your advice, but you're dead wrong on this one. Charlie would drive me nuts within a week, and you'd find me on your doorstep in Japan begging you to hide me." Davis smiled and relaxed a little as they moved on. "But I'll keep an eye out for someone who might suit me. I never said I wouldn't. Those long cold nights would be warmer in front of a crackling fire with a wife and a couple of kids."

"As long as you're keeping an open mind, then I'll close my mouth. I really did think you and Charlie hit it off, the way the two of you were going at each other. One thing you can say for her, she doesn't blend into the woodwork."

"You're right there. Whenever she's around, I feel like we're back in grade school, taking turns sticking toads in each other's desks." Davis grimaced. "While I appreciate your wanting to look out for me, I have something a little different in mind when choosing a wife."

When Charlie got to the mall, the clock was just chiming eleven o'clock. Up ahead, she saw someone whose back closely resembled Davis's. But it couldn't be him, could it? The man was dressed in a designer suit, like Davis. And like Davis, he wore cowboy boots.

Accompanying him was a gentleman who bore a striking resemblance to Jim Turner. Was it possible she'd run into them?

She watched them casually stroll toward a jewelry store and was rewarded with the men's profiles as they studied the window offerings. It *was* Davis and Jim.

Charlie wondered whether she should head the other way or greet them. Hiding was tempting, but if she tried that, she was certain to be caught.

As she walked up to join them, Jim pointed out a ring, but Davis shook his head.

"Shopping for yourselves, gentlemen, or for a gift?" she asked.

"Hi, Charlie," said Davis with a friendly smile. "What are you doing here?"

"Heavy dress shopping again," she said. "When I buy one, do you want still to carry it?"

Davis gave her a sheepish grin. "If you'd like."

Jim turned and greeted her with a firm handshake. "I think you got here just in time. Davis doesn't like any of the engagement rings I've pointed out. I think the two of you should select one together."

"Well, an idea did occur to me." She wasn't quite sure whether Davis would like the idea, but it would salve her conscience as well as save him money.

"Good," said Jim. "I'll leave you to it."

"Wait a sec," said Charlie, but Jim dashed off down the mall before either of them could stop him.

Charlie laughed. "You must have been making a real chore out of ring shopping, Davis."

"Somehow I think this is your fault more than my own," he replied. "This ring business is difficult. Why don't I give you my credit card and—"

"If we're back to that, I won't tell you about my wonderful idea." Charlie tossed her head.

"So, what's your idea?"

"Are you through blaming things on me?"

Davis sighed. "I won't blame you anymore. Now, what's your idea?"

She bit her lip, then slowly grinned. "Well, there's this knock-off store here, on the upper level of the mall. It's got rhinestone and cubic zirconia copies of the big-name designer rings, set in gold. They're cheap and they look real. We could get something really showy for about five hundred dollars. What do you think?"

"No fiancée of mine would wear paste."

"Oh, it's not paste. After our engagement is over, I won't feel bad about keeping the ring. What do you say?"

"I suppose it won't hurt to look." Davis set his jaw in a stubborn expression. "But if they look fake, I'm going to buy you the real thing. You can keep it anyway."

"There's no need to buy real diamonds, since our engagement is as phony as the knock-off rings."

Davis had to hand it to Charlie. She even made jewelry stores fun. By the time they'd finally settled on the perfect engagement ring, she had everyone in the store laughing, including a couple of society matrons who'd been trying to shield their identities.

As he paid for the ring, Charlie stood outside the shop in conversation with a library patron. Earlier, Davis had seen a rhinestone pin shaped like a cowboy hat. He grabbed it and purchased it as well.

After the sales clerk gave him his bag with the two jewelry boxes tucked neatly inside, Davis rejoined Charlie outside the store. "Do you have time for some lunch?"

"Not really, but we do need to talk. Your mom called today."

"She did?"

"She invited me to her bridal shower this evening."

As they talked, they descended the escalator and found a quiet table on the edge of the food court. Davis pulled out her chair. Once she was seated, he took a chair of his own. "I'm sorry this is turning into a lot more than I'd originally asked."

"Me, too. I feel as if I have the word 'fraud' stamped on my forehead." Charlie shook her head. "Maybe I shouldn't go this weekend, after all."

Davis's heart sank. She was right—he kept asking more and more of her and it really wasn't fair. "All I wanted was to see Mom happy."

Charlie reached out and patted his hand. "I know. I have to admit, I want her happy, too. But this is all more involved than I'd imagined."

He held himself totally still. If Charlie backed out now, what would his mother do? Would she go through with marrying Jim? Would she ever speak to Davis again? Not wanting to give away how important it was to him, he tried to keep all expression from his face and voice as he asked, "Are you saying you can't go through with this?"

Charlie lowered her head. "I don't know."

He breathed in a quick breath. So it wasn't hopeless. He remembered the mailbox, the cupid, the laughter in the jewelry store. "We've had a lot of fun, haven't we?"

She looked up, smiling. "Yes."

"Charlie—" Would it be fair to beg her to keep up the ruse? Most of all, he didn't want to stop seeing her. Somehow, she'd worked her elfin magic, and he'd spent the entire week thinking about her silly dimple. How she'd have appreciated a joke or rolled her eyes at something someone said. How he felt on top of the world when he was with her. If it took begging, he'd do it. "It wouldn't be for much longer, and means a lot to my mom." It did to him, too, but he couldn't admit it.

"So I suppose I have to attend the shower tonight." Charlie sighed, then gave him a resigned expression. "I'll stop in and leave early."

"Thanks." He opened the bag and pulled out the jewelry boxes. "Guess we'd better make this official."

"Don't even think about it," she growled.

Davis flipped open the ring box. "Think about what?"

"Don't get any ideas that this is anything more than a temporary engagement, as we originally agreed. No more, no less."

Again, Davis froze. Did she mean that if he was seriously offering to marry her that she'd say no? He honestly believed she was attracted to him. What was it about him that she found so wrong? He bit back a taste of irritation. It wasn't as if he'd even asked.

But it sure would be nice to receive reassurance that he hadn't lost his touch. Pulling the ring from the box, he gently clasped her hand in his, then tugged it to his lips and brushed a kiss on it.

He slowly slid the ring onto her finger, drawing out the moment as much as he dared, hoping his hands weren't shaking. He looked deeply into her eyes, and his voice came out husky as he whispered, "Be mine."

Charlie blinked, then yanked back her hand. "What?"

"That ring should do just fine." Davis grinned as she searched his expression suspiciously, once more reassured that the attraction still lay there between them.

He slid the other box in front of her. "I got you something else for being such a good sport."

A light of pleasure lit her face as she gazed up at him, making her eyes sparkle like sunlight on water. "What is it?"

"Open it and find out."

She deftly flipped the box lid open, revealing the pin he'd bought. The light seemed to die in her eyes. "Thank you, Davis." She scooped the boxes back into the bag lying on the table between them, then rose. "I have to go now."

She didn't think she could bear being with him another second, much less for the weekend she'd promised. She'd almost allowed him to pierce her armor, but his gift had recalled her just in the nick of time.

"Wait a sec, Charlie. What on earth went wrong?"

"Nothing went wrong." She looked at him defiantly. "You merely reminded me of why there can never be anything between us."

"What did I do?"

"It's not what you did, Davis. It's who you are." She turned to walk away.

"The fact that I'm a bachelor makes me ineligible?"

Facing him, her heart pounded. "No. The fact that you're a cowboy, or the next thing to it."

With that, she walked off, not wanting to prolong the discussion, not wanting to face him and have to explain any further. Talking about it wouldn't make her feel any differently—she'd never allow herself to fall in love with a cowboy. It was her own fault that she kept forgetting Davis intended to become one.

Chapter Six

Charlie scooted out of her car, carrying the shower gift she'd purchased for Ellen. She was a quarter of an hour late, having left the library early to buy the gift and a dress to wear in the wedding.

She was pleased with both of her purchases. For Ellen, she'd bought an attractive dressing case, outfitted with plenty of bottles for filling with shampoo and soaps, and lots of little boxes for organizing makeup and jewelry.

For herself, Charlie had bought a blue dress. The color matched her eyes, and the lines of the dress were deceptively simple. It would be perfect for the wedding, and practical in that she'd be able to wear it to work.

Now, all she had to do was get through the next

few days and all this fiancée business would be over with. Entering the office, a middle-aged woman greeted her.

"Hi, you must be Charlie. Let me take that package. I'm Lily."

"Hi, Lily. It's nice to meet you." They quickly shook hands, then Lily led her back to the conference room.

On the way there, Charlie looked around her. While the company looked like a typical office, many of the furnishings and wall hangings had a western flavor. Typical.

When they reached the conference room, there were about half a dozen women gathered around a long marble table. Centered on the table was a lovely flower arrangement. In the far corner stood a narrow wooden table where cake and refreshments had been laid out. Ellen stood there, in quiet discussion with another woman.

Lily announced brightly, "Look who's here, ladies! Charlie Nelson, Davis's fiancée. I'll let you all introduce yourselves after I get her some punch."

Ellen came over and hugged Charlie. "Thanks so much for coming, dear."

Before she had time to answer, the woman Ellen had been speaking with joined them, cooing, "Let me see your ring!"

The next thing she knew, she was surrounded by women, chattering and asking questions.

"Have you known each other long?"

"How many carats is it?"

"How did you get him to pop the question?"

"Where does your family come from?"

"Let me get you some punch—"

"cake—"

"chips."

Charlie's head swam. She grabbed a seat at the conference table and did her best to answer everyone. It was hard to keep up, however, and at some point, the conversation had changed when she hadn't been paying close enough attention. Now they were talking about—wedding nights? Or perhaps giving her advice?

She wasn't sure.

"You know dear," assured one woman, "men have to be trained, just like any household pet. It's up to the woman to lay down the rules from the beginning."

Lily piped in. "The main thing you have to teach a man is that timing is everything."

"Timing." Charlie nodded as if she understood what Lily meant. She didn't, but she wasn't sure if she wanted to, either.

A dignified matron from the other side of the table nodded her head sagely. "We want to know all about you, dear."

After another round of questions, Charlie asked, "How do each of you know Davis? It seems—"

Her question was cut off by the opening of the conference room door. Davis poked his head in.

Ellen literally jumped out of her chair and dragged him into the room.

"I came to kidnap my fiancée. You guys about done?"

Ellen nodded. "I think Charlie's had enough of Fifty Questions."

Once they had escaped, and walked to the parking lot, Davis said, "I thought you might need some help in there."

"You're right, I did. But they're all very fond of you."

"I'm fond of them, too." They reached her car. Davis asked, "Want to grab a bite to eat?"

"No, but thanks for asking."

"How about if I drive you home?"

"I'm fine, Davis."

"It's too late for you to be out driving alone. I think I should drive you. Give me your keys."

"I've been driving myself alone at night for years. You're being awfully bossy, acting like a typical man."

"I know." Davis nodded gravely. "Like most men, it's one of my worst character flaws."

"You won't get an argument from me."

"Good, because you're about to learn about another of my character flaws."

"Oh, yeah?"

He nodded. "And remember, you're the one who said there'd be no arguing."

With that, he lowered his head and kissed her.

The following afternoon, Charlie busily packed her suitcase for the weekend at the lake. She tossed in jeans, a heavy windbreaker, her bridesmaid dress, and another dress in case they went out to dinner somewhere.

Joanne leaned against the doorjamb, overseeing. "You might want to add a bottle of aspirin, considering your reaction every time you've seen Davis."

"Very funny." Charlie threw in the aspirin, though, as advised. "So, I kissed the man. Again. I'll be on guard not to let it happen anymore."

"Right."

"And no matter what he thinks, he's not my knight in shining stirrups."

"Whatever you say," said Joanne, grinning ear to ear.

"And no matter what *you* say, I was *not* singing in the shower this morning." Charlie grabbed her makeup bag off her dresser. "I *never* sing in the shower."

Joanne snickered. "Must have been that new love song radio station, WLUV."

Charlie laid her makeup bag back on the dresser and leaned toward her reflection in the mirror. She caught Joanne's gaze. "I didn't really sing *love* songs?"

Joanne nodded.

"I think I need to sit." Charlie sank onto her bed next to her suitcase, sending two pairs of socks tumbling to the floor. "I am *not* in love with him."

Joanne laughed. "Don't worry, honey. It was just a kiss."

"You're right."

Joanne waltzed from the room, but called over her shoulder, "By the way, you had a delivery this morning."

"What is it?"

"You'll have to find out for yourself. It's in the kitchen," said Joanne as she walked away.

Charlie wondered what it could be as she placed the makeup bag into her suitcase, fighting the urge to rush into the kitchen; that was exactly the reaction Joanne was hoping for. But Charlie was on a mission to break out of her old routine.

So she'd kissed Davis. It didn't mean anything. He was always trying to kiss her. She was not going to fall in love with a cowboy. She snapped her suitcase closed.

In the big scheme of things, a kiss or two was not of earth-shattering importance. She'd just have to make sure that there wouldn't be a repeat.

She tried to work up some justifiable anger, but there wasn't any excuse for her behavior. Worrying about it wouldn't get her anywhere. She'd just have to make the rules more clear to Davis. Sometimes, with men, she'd found it helped to be extremely explicit.

Turning, she checked herself in the mirror. Blue jeans, a sky-blue button-down polo shirt. Would she be warm enough? She opened her closet door and pulled out a red sweater. That should do it.

She was as ready as she'd ever be, wasn't she? Charlie looked back over her room, feeling as if she'd forgotten something, reluctant to leave. She didn't see anything out of place.

Then she remembered the delivery Joanne had mentioned.

She found it on the kitchen counter. A cut-glass vase held a single daisy, and tucked beneath it looked like a note. Charlie picked it up. It read: *I'm looking forward to this weekend*. It was signed simply, *Davis*.

Why did he have to be so nice?

* * *

"When I agreed to come to Lake Texoma, I thought we'd be *driving*, like normal people." Charlie strapped on her safety belt and looked out of the small plane at the runway. She felt thoroughly irritated.

Now she sat beside him in a midget of an airplane of all things. He did look kind of cute, clad in a leather bomber jacket, jeans and a headphone. The man was big on wearing the appropriate apparel. She checked his feet. Some things never changed— he still wore cowboy boots.

When she first realized he meant to fly to the lake, she'd thought of backing out. She wouldn't be a coward, though. She'd promised herself to stop living life in the safe lane.

"Normal people also fly," said Davis.

"Not the normal people I know. They use commercial airlines with real planes, not Tinker Toys. Are you certain you're licensed for this?"

He looked at her with wide eyes. "You need a license to fly one of these?"

"I knew it." Charlie threw off her seatbelt and struggled to get out of her seat. "I knew I should never have let some sweet-talking cowboy convince me to do anything so stupid."

Davis flipped down a visor, then pointed out a certificate bearing his name. His license.

"I should get out of this clump of metal and go

home. That's what any sane woman would do." Charlie plopped back down and rebuckled her belt.

"Sanity is overrated."

"Ha! I've survived quite well with a combination of sanity and common sense. And survival is uppermost in my mind right now. Where are the parachutes?"

Davis gave her hand a reassuring squeeze.

Charlie relaxed in spite of herself. She'd been dreading this trip all week, wondering if she'd be tongue-tied, wondering how she felt about this maddening man, sometimes forgetting he was a cowboy and other times furious because he was. And there was the daisy.

"Thanks for the flower." She had to shout to be heard over the sound of the revving motors. "Why did you send it?"

"You're welcome. It's time to get ready for takeoff." Davis looked uncomfortable for a moment as he fidgeted with some gauges and dials. He adjusted his headset, then handed one to her. "Put it on."

"Why?"

"So we can hear each other."

"Oh." Charlie slipped it over her head, feeling foolish.

Davis pulled back the throttle, and suddenly the plane bumped into motion, taxiing down the runway. After takeoff, he pointed out a few sights, and flew as low over Addison, the north Dallas suburb in which the small private airport was located, as the flight controllers would allow. Charlie craned her neck to take in the high-rise buildings.

He wasn't entirely sure himself why he'd sent her the flower. He'd done it because he thought she'd like it, but that wasn't it entirely. After they'd parted the night before, he'd been unable to get her out of his mind. When had pleasing her become so important to him?

She'd climbed under his skin in a way no other woman had, and he wasn't sure what he thought or how he felt about it.

He didn't like feeling confused or out of control. Somehow he had to keep in mind that their relationship was temporary, and she was only going to be around long enough to help him get his mother married off. It was time to relegate Charlie to the same status he'd always held other women: at arm's length.

Joanne ran from the bathroom and answered the phone on the third ring. With Charlie out of town for the weekend, she had planned an intimate dinner party: just her and the man of her dreams. She hoped it wasn't him on the phone, telling her there'd be some delay. She didn't think the Cornish game hens could wait.

She had to angle the receiver just right because her hot curlers interfered. "Hello?"

"Hey, Joanne. This is Monty Joe. How you doin', girl?"

Joanne let out a sigh of relief. It was just Charlie's brother calling to check on her. Joanne's dinner could still go as planned. If she wasn't seriously involved with Mike, she'd consider pursuing one of Charlie's brothers. They were incredibly good-looking, even if they leaned a little to the macho side. "I'm doing fine, how about you and Bobby Gray?"

"We're doin' just fine. We've taken it into our heads to come to Dallas and see our little sister. Put her on, will you?"

"I'm sorry, but she's not here." Joanne sniffed the air. Smoke? Something was burning—she hoped it was dinner and not her hair. *Dinner!* "Look, I have to get to the kitchen. Charlie's gone to Lake Texoma and won't be back until Sunday night."

"Lake Texoma? What's she doing there?"

Smoke wafted out of the bar area. The Cornish hens must be burning. "Don't worry. She's in good hands. She went with Davis Murphy."

"Hold on there a minute!"

"Hang on a sec. Dinner's burning!" She threw down the receiver and ran into the kitchen, then pulled open the oven door. Sure enough the hens were overdone, but she thought they might still be salvageable. She pulled them out of the oven and turned on the exhaust fan.

Returning to the phone, she said, "I really can't talk now, Monty Joe. I've got a date coming over and dinner is almost ruined."

"Do you know where 'bouts at the lake she's headed?"

Joanne wanted to scream with frustration. Here he was, asking her fifty questions, when she had hens to salvage. And if Mike arrived with her hair still up in curlers, she looked such a fright he might run for the hills. "She wrote down the phone number here somewhere . . ."

Chapter Seven

"About this fiancée business," said Charlie as Davis switched on the autopilot. "I'm a little nervous about this weekend."

"I'm sure you'll do fine," said Davis.

"But how should I act around your family and friends?"

"Well, let me think." Now that the autopilot was in control, there was less risk of him becoming distracted enough to do anything stupid. He could turn his attention totally to Charlie.

Why was it that all his male antennae went into high gear whenever she was near? If he was honest with himself, he had to admit it happened just by thinking about her. When had he become so intrigued by her?

And looking at her expectant face now, as she waited for him to reassure her, made him feel protective. A lock of her hair, resembling a loose corkscrew, had settled over her left eye. He'd seen that before and had tucked it behind her ear. This time, though, he didn't. She just looked so darn cute, just like an elf, as he'd taken to calling her, not at like women he'd been interested in before.

Even in a drafty airplane, he could smell that scent of hers, sort of an old-fashioned type of fragrance—like old lace and spring flowers.

What was he going to do about her? Perhaps instead of avoiding her, he should spend more time with her. If they were together enough, he'd grow tired of her company and he'd seek the solitude he generally craved. "I think it best if you stick close by this weekend."

"Stay near you?"

Davis nodded. What else? Something to speed things along. If he kissed her enough, surely he'd become immune? "While I'll admit it's probably my fault for choosing a woman who has no fiancée experience, with someone as intelligent as you, I don't think you'll need much by way of instruction."

"That wasn't quite what I meant." She crinkled her nose, doing strange things to his stomach, and making him want to laugh. When she got prissy, some inner part of him delighted in it. Like a challenge that had to be acted on, he was compelled to break through her attitude.

"I thought you wanted some lessons on the appropriate behavior of an engaged woman."

"You did, did you?" asked Charlie through gritted teeth. "First you get me into this death trap, and now this."

"I don't know what I said that's got you riled up." He gave her his most disarming grin. The prissier she became, the greater the challenge.

"While I'll be the first to admit I've never been engaged before, I certainly feel I have a good handle on how an engaged woman should behave." Charlie batted her eyelashes at him. "What exactly is it you think I need to learn?"

This was more like it. "Well, as my intended, you have to get used to being kissed. Often. No use getting worked up over it, my family and friends expect me to kiss my fiancée."

Charlie snorted. "I already figured that one out."

"Atta girl."

He heard a hissing noise from Charlie's direction, but when he looked at her, she smiled innocently.

"Now," continued Davis. "I'm not one to spoil fun, but I do expect you to be around, to be at hand should I need you. What I have in mind is a little concern about my welfare."

"Obviously I'd be concerned about your welfare."

"You won't want to overdo it, but if you're off chatting with someone, it just won't do."

"Okay, we already covered me staying close to you. I don't see what the problem is, though."

Davis schooled his expression, to make sure she wouldn't see how amused he was. "The problem would be, you won't be there to fetch me a soda or laugh at my jokes." That should be almost guaranteed to rile her.

"You want me to fetch you drinks?"

Davis nodded.

"You want me to fawn over you?"

"Fawning might be too much, but I imagine my fiancée would be concerned about whether I was having a good time. And you need to stay far away from the single guys." Pulling her leg was one heck of a lot of fun. Any second now, she'd go ballistic.

"I don't know how to tell you this, but what you want is a wet nurse, not a fiancée." She threw up her arms. "Men!"

"Now hold on a second—I didn't say that."

"Nonsense. You think anyone will believe you care about a woman whose sole purpose in life is to cater to your over-inflated ego? Do you really think you'd respect that kind of woman? I wouldn't."

"We're not talking respect here. We're talking the kind of woman who'd steal my heart and make me give up a very peaceful bachelor existence." This was better than stealing candy from a baby. "If my fiancée is off having a good time and I'm nowhere near, how does that make me look?"

"Like you're in love?"

"Heck, no. It makes me look like a fool, wrapped around some woman's pinky while she kicks up her heels."

"All I can tell you is, I'm not that kind of woman. Since it's too late for you to switch fiancées, you'll have to put up with what you've got, because there's no way I'm going to act like the bimbos you seem to find acceptable as marriage material."

"You won't go along like a good sport?"

"No, I won't." Her voice was as calm as a tornado's eye.

"You'll make a fool out of me."

"No. Love makes everyone act like fools. If you want to be believable, you'll have to take my word on this one."

Davis couldn't hold his laughter in another minute. He cracked up.

"You've been teasing me, haven't you?" asked Charlie suspiciously, a smile playing about her lips.

"I'm sorry, but you're hilarious when you get up on your high horse."

"Hilarious. Ha ha." Charlie swatted his arm. "I was serious. I need to know how to act."

"Okay. Here's my idea. You don't fetch me sodas, but I expect calf-eyes from you."

"You got it. When we're standing on the opposite side of the same room, I'll remember to look at you worshipfully."

"That's good." He wiggled his eyebrows. "Look at me like I'm your personal gift from heaven. And when we're near . . ."

The look he sent her almost made her forget what they were talking about.

She gulped.

This was getting better, closer to his goal. "My mother will expect me to kiss you. A lot."

A flush rose across her neck and face and she wouldn't meet his gaze.

He patted her hand. "Don't worry. I'll help you along."

That was exactly what she feared. For all his conceit, she did feel attracted to him. He was good-looking and gifted with charm, and he used it to get his own way. *In fact,* she shot him a suspicious glance, *hadn't he just had his way now? More kisses? Two could play this game.* "I want to add a stipulation."

"What's that?"

"No more kisses when no one is watching."

"We've got to practice."

"I think we've practiced just about enough."

He leaned forward, as if he were about to kiss her again. She held up her hand.

"I mean it, Davis." This would be the only way she'd be able to remember the difference between her role and reality. If his intentions were honorable, she'd eat his Stetson. This was the only way to protect herself.

"I'm not making any promises. What if you asked me to kiss you?"

"I won't."

"Here's what I'll agree to. All you have to do is tell me to stop, and I will. Deal?"

"I thought our deal was for me to pretend to be your fiancée? I think I'm more than satisfying those requirements."

"What are you afraid of, Charlie? That you'll forget to say *no*?"

"Of course not!" It wasn't what she wanted, but it seemed the best she could get him to agree to. He might be a Romeo, but she knew she could trust him to stop if she told him to. "You've got a deal."

Davis grinned. Something about his self-satisfaction again reminded her of her brothers' prize bull. Suspecting she'd been outmaneuvered, she narrowed her eyes at him, but he was busy fidgeting with dials and gauges, and talking into his radio.

"We're about to land."

Sure enough, he was bringing the plane down. As he landed the aircraft, Charlie was surprised that he didn't head for an airport. Instead, he settled the plane on a small landing strip, then taxied to a stop on the grass.

He killed the engine and helped her disembark. "The house isn't far."

She looked around. Trees and grass were the only things visible for what appeared to be miles. "You've got to be kidding."

"Nope, it's just behind that hill." Davis pointed to a small incline. "I'll come back for our bags later."

Charlie looked in that direction. She saw cypresses, but there wasn't even a clear path that she could make out. Shrugging, she followed him across the field and to the trees. Sure enough, as he'd promised, she saw a house just down the slope. Behind the house to the right about two hundred feet, she saw a pier which led to a gazebo which appeared to be floating on the lake. On the water toward the left rear of the house was a metal boathouse. The view was breathtaking. In the background, she heard the sound of waves lapping against the beach and the drone of a motorboat in the distance.

It was quiet, peaceful, the type of place she imagined when life became too stressful. Closing her eyes for a moment, she allowed the call of the water to wash over her, bathe her in its tranquil harmony. "No wonder your mom wanted to get married here. It's beautiful."

"Jim said I can use it as much as I'd like while he's out of the country. Of course, with my job and trying to buy a ranch, I don't know how often I'll be able to make it up here."

"How did you come to run Murphy Title when your heart isn't in it?" Charlie drank in the view as they got closer. The house wasn't large, but it was quaint, with a huge bow window overlooking the woods and grassy field, and the gravel driveway leading up to it. It was a narrow house, with white clapboard and black shutters, and two stories tall. Yet despite being made by man and not by nature, it seemed to fit into this setting as if it had been planned from the beginning of time.

"When my father died, the company wasn't in good shape. The real estate market was at an all-time low, and there wasn't much call for warranties or titles. As soon as I finished school, I took it over. I had to look after Mom and make sure she didn't lose her home. For a while, it was questionable, and I despaired of ever learning the business. It wasn't easy. Finally my hard work is paying off."

"From what I understand, you've done very well."

"I've done my best, and I think it's strong enough to continue without me now. So I'm scouting around for a ranch to buy."

"Well, I wish you luck. All I've ever wanted was to stay as far away from a ranch as possible. If I had the use of this place, I'd never want to leave." She understood wanting something you couldn't have, but she couldn't understand why he was so fixated on being a cowboy. "Wouldn't you like to explore the world?"

Davis shrugged. "Traveling is okay, but most big cities are pretty much like every other. And a hotel is a hotel is a hotel. No, I've almost got the opportunity to do something I've always wanted. Raise some cattle, maybe even show some. And there's one thing I intend to do."

"What's that?"

"Ride in the rodeo. Like my grandfather."

Warning bells went off in her head. First of all it was dangerous. And second of all, he was too old. Ridiculous cowboy! He'd kill himself. But that was one thing he certainly had in common with all the other cowboys she'd ever met. They were thrill-seekers, risking life and limb, breaking the hearts of their loved ones. All for what? A chance at winning a purse of $5,000 or less?

Idiots. All of them, chasing after some shiny brass buckle to wear on their belts. And Davis was no different. From now on, she wouldn't forget again. No more kisses unless there was an audience—no hand-holding, either. She'd keep her distance and her heart safe. "You'll be lucky if you don't break your neck."

"I'll be extremely cautious."

"How many times have I heard that before?" Charlie asked under her breath. As they neared the house, she saw a narrow inlet of water off to her left, leading to the lake. "I hope you know what you're doing."

"I've done a lot of studying and spend most of my spare time practicing."

"Uh huh." *Men!* Exasperating fools. His idea of practicing and hers were most likely worlds apart.

Just then, Davis surprised her again by pulling her into his arms. He ran his thumb over her bottom lip and gazed fully into her eyes.

"Who's watching?"

"I saw someone standing near the house. It could be my mother. Just follow my lead, okay?"

Charlie nodded. Telling herself he was a cowboy didn't seem to do the trick. Her heart pounded as he lowered his head toward hers. He might have had to study ranching, but he sure didn't need instruction when it came to kissing. And thoughts like that were what tended to get her in trouble.

She shook herself free. Blinking in the brilliant sunlight, she focused on the house. Sure enough, he was trying to trick her again. There was no one within sight. "Your mother?"

"Looks like I was mistaken."

"You're darn right you were mistaken." Very deliberately, she gave him a shove, neatly toppling him, bottom first, into the inlet of water.

After Davis had sloshed his way through the house and shown Charlie where her bedroom was, he dripped his way into the kitchen. There he found Jim on the phone.

Jim waved to him but continued talking to whomever was on the line. "Yeah, we'll expect you then. Looking forward to it." After hanging up the receiver, he turned to Davis. "You and Charlie all settled?"

"Yes, I put her in the room at the end of the hall. I hope that's right?"

"That's where Ellen planned." Jim's brows creased as his gaze centered on the puddle at Davis's feet. "Did you have an accident?"

"Just took a little dip," replied Davis. No need to give the man any more ammunition than he already had.

Chapter Eight

Charlie opened her suitcase and began to unpack. Her room had two twin beds and a small dresser. While not decorated in the height of style, it was attractive and clean.

She pulled out her bridesmaid dress first. After checking it for wrinkles, she hung it in the closet, glad it had traveled so well. As she returned to the case, she burrowed around in her belongings, unable to spot the lavender dress she'd stuck in at the last moment. It wasn't here.

Then her gaze settled on something red at the bottom of the case. Joanne hadn't . . . she had. It was apparent that she had removed the lavender dress and replaced it with The Dress. Now what was Charlie going to do?

Tonight they were having a rehearsal, then going to dinner. Besides the two dresses, she'd only brought casual clothes. Charlie noticed that Joanne had even thought to include her awful matching shoes. If she were here now, Charlie would definitely consider choking her.

There was nothing to do but to wear the dreaded red dress again. The one she'd promised herself she'd avoid. She laid it out on her bed and finished unpacking, every movement she made drawing her attention back to the dress. When she'd procrastinated as long as she could, arranging her hair brush and refolding her clothes, she took a seat on her bed.

"You're to blame, you know." Charlie glared at the dress. "I just wanted to take one small step, and you turned it into an earthquake. I was never going to wear you again, but I don't have a choice tonight. Please behave yourself. I don't want more trouble."

The dress seemed to mock her, but she didn't have a choice.

Once she'd gotten dressed and buoyed her courage, Charlie went to the family room to find Davis. He was sitting with his back to her, facing the fireplace. Gentle flames highlighted his black hair, lighting it almost like a halo. Fat chance—Davis was no angel.

"Hi," she said softly.

"You look great tonight, Charlie," he said, before he'd fully turned around. Then he saw her completely and the smile died from his face, replaced with a look of admiration. Under his gaze, she fought an urge to return to her room and hide. But then he gave her a boyish grin and she relaxed.

"I see you're wearing my favorite dress."

"It *would* be your favorite—this dress is the root of all my problems."

"You look fantastic in it. But you look great no matter what."

"Thanks, I'll remember that the next time I have a bad hair day." She fought back a snort. The cad. He was feeding her ego, using his charm on her. But deep down inside, she appreciated the effort. He didn't have to say nice things when they were alone, but he did. Even though it was probably habit, it was a nice habit. "Where are the others?"

"They're out in the gazebo, talking with Judge Hawkins about how to organize things. You ready?"

"Yes. Do you think I'll be warm enough?"

"You might want to bring a sweater for when it gets dark, but it's still warm now."

"I'll get it." Maybe wearing the sweater would impair the dress's ability to cause trouble. She ran to her room and put the sweater on before returning. She didn't look exactly like a fashion plate, but she'd be warm.

As she rejoined Davis, she said, "I'm ready."

He took her hand as they went through the glass doors that led out onto the deck facing the lake. His palm was clammy, moist. "Are you nervous?"

"Yeah." He grimaced. "I think weddings make me hyperventilate."

"Maybe you should bring a paper sack?"

"No." He gave her hand a squeeze. "I'll be fine. If I'm not, just make sure you're the one who gives me mouth-to-mouth."

They walked down the lawn to the pier. As they climbed onto the dock, Charlie's stiletto heel caught in a gap between the slats. "I think I wore the wrong shoes for this."

"You want to go back and change shoes?"

"All I've got are sneakers or my blue flats for tomorrow." She shook her head. "I think I'll be okay if I'm careful."

He put his arm around her back. "Lean on me if you have problems."

Charlie nodded. It was about all she could manage, while she fought the urge to pull away and the urge to put her head on his shoulder.

They slowly made their way to the gazebo, Charlie careful to put her weight only on her toes. Davis's arm helped steady her.

The gazebo was roughly twenty feet in diameter, large enough to hold the small wedding party planned for the next day, but without a lot of room to spare. Along the outer edges, wooden benches were built into the latticework, and would serve as seating for the guests. The gazebo sported huge blue and yellow satin bows with sprays of baby's breath accenting them. It was an ideal spot for a wedding.

But nothing could have been more lovely than the sight of Jim and Ellen's jubilant faces. They stood with the judge in the middle of the gazebo, talking about their plans following the wedding. "We'll stay in town to finish last-minute arrangements and leave for Tokyo next Saturday," said Jim.

Ellen noticed Charlie and Davis first. "There you two lovebirds are! I thought we were going to have to send out a search party."

Davis grinned. "I wouldn't miss this for anything, Mom."

Ellen gave them each a hug. "I'm getting so excited. I can't believe this is really happening."

The judge and Jim laughed. "Yeah, we've been teasing her about tying an anchor to her feet to keep her head from floating into the clouds."

"I'm so happy." She smiled widely.

Jim brushed a quick kiss on her cheek. "No one could be happier than me." He turned to the judge. "Let's get this show on the road so I can toast my bride."

For the next quarter hour, Ellen and Charlie practiced walking down the pier and to the middle of the gazebo. They were told where to stand and what to do. Gradually, the sun dipped over the quiet lake, beaming a huge orange slash across the blackening water, like an arrow directing the heavens to the gazebo and the wedding preparations within.

As the sky darkened, overhead lighting flashed on, illuminating not only the gazebo and pier but the beach and the boathouse. As they practiced their walk to the gazebo for the third time, Ellen suggested that Charlie and Davis sit the next part out because Charlie's shoes made movement difficult.

"Good idea," agreed Charlie. "I'm sorry about the shoes."

"It's no problem. If it were, I'd send Davis to the house for your sneakers. We've got the main part rehearsed, and once we practice the ceremony, we can head for the marina restaurant."

Charlie took a step closer to the gazebo, silently counting out one-kick, two-kick, three-kick in her head. Then another step, but this time, she misstepped, her shoe becoming hopelessly trapped between the slats. "Ow. I twisted my ankle."

Ellen came running forward. "Can you get your shoe off?"

Charlie nodded. "I think so." She bent to unstrap the shoe but had a hard time maintaining her balance.

Ellen called out, "Davis, we could use your help."

Both Davis and Jim came running up the pier. Davis had a worried expression on his face as he asked, "Are you hurt, Charlie?"

"No, I'm okay, just trapped."

Davis bent over her shoe and quickly unbuckled it.

Charlie giggled. "Ever since you saw these shoes, you've been dying to do that."

"Yeah," he agreed. "Finally, my chance." He stuck the shoe in his pocket.

Charlie wiggled her ankle.

"Does it hurt?" asked Jim.

"Just a little—more sore than painful."

Davis scooped her up in his arms. "I'll carry you back to the house."

"I'm perfectly capable of walking."

"Maybe so, but we want you fit for the wedding tomorrow."

Ellen said, "I agree with him, Charlie. The less you use it now, the better it will be for tomorrow."

"But the rehearsal . . ."

Jim said, "We're about done with your part, and just have to go over the bride and groom parts now."

Charlie looked up at Davis, annoyed with him for being so quick to grab her into his arms, and yet breathless at being there. "I don't want to miss it."

"Don't worry." Davis nodded toward the deck off the back of the house. "I'll get some ice for your ankle and we can sit up there and watch. You won't miss anything."

"Thanks." Charlie turned back to Ellen and Jim. "I'm sorry about this."

"Just relax, dear. It's fine." Ellen laughed as Davis adjusted Charlie's weight in his arms. "You'd better get her back to the house before you drop her in the water."

Davis laughed. "Good thinking."

Before she knew it, Charlie was seated in a deck chair, watching the wedding rehearsal from a distance. The deck and house behind them were dark, the only light coming from down by the water. Davis had pulled another deck chair to her side and placed her foot on it, mounded with ice. He took a seat next to her and brought them each a steaming cup of hot tea laden with cream.

"Why don't you go back down and help? I'm just fine here."

"They don't need us. The rehearsal is almost over."

Ellen waved at them from the gazebo and both Jim and the judge turned and waved, too. Everything was fine.

At least tonight, thought Charlie, the dress hadn't

done the damage. Only the shoes were a problem and it was my own fault for wearing them.

She took a sip of her tea, breathing in the creamy aroma and the mists of the evening sky. The house behind them was cloaked in darkness but the night sky was lit up like a million fireflies. The moon was just past full, its light reflecting off the inky water. Davis leaned his head back too, gazing into the night.

"You know," he said, "This is just about perfect. All those stars—and you." Davis felt content. When was the last time he'd taken the time to soak in the beauty of his surroundings?

His life, and his goals, had always been there to hurry him, to rush him. He'd forgotten the simple pleasures. Being with Charlie acted as a catalyst. He was more aware when she was with him, his vision stronger, aromas more pungent. Taste took on new meaning, and touch . . .

He leaned closer. "I'm going to kiss you. Stop me while you can."

She placed her arm around his shoulder and neck, drawing him nearer as she returned his kiss.

Just then, he heard a masculine cough. Davis opened his eyes and looked up.

Two burly men glared down at him.

Chapter Nine

"What are you doing here, Monty Joe and Bobby Gray?" exclaimed Charlie as she bolted from the deck chair.

Davis stood, shot a questioning glance at Charlie, then offered his hand to Monty Joe. "Davis Murphy."

"In case you were wondering, they are my brothers." She turned to face them. "I'm asking again, what are you doing here?"

"Joanne told us everything—that you took off with some guy for the weekend. When we called, it sounded like some tryst. We came to make you come to your senses."

Bobby Gray glared at her. "Looks like we got here just in the nick of time, too."

"Don't be ridiculous," said Charlie. "I'm not a child anymore, and it's time you stopped treating me like one. If I want to run off with a man, then it's *my* business, not yours."

"You said it, sweetie," said Ellen from behind Charlie.

"Yeah, can you believe these guys?" she asked without thinking.

"Who are they?" asked Ellen.

"My brothers." Then it dawned on her—Ellen was witnessing the whole thing. She turned to face her. "I'm so sorry. I was hoping they'd go before you saw them. It's a disgrace."

Jim coughed. "Glad to see your brothers made it here okay."

"Your directions were excellent, Jim," said Bobby Gray.

"Have you met?" asked Davis.

"No. We spoke on the phone." Monty Joe looked at Jim suspiciously. "We appreciate the invite."

"In that case," said Charlie, "I'd like to introduce you to our chaperones—Davis's mother, Ellen Murphy, and Jim Turner, her fiancé."

Judge Hawkins leaned around Jim to add, "Don't forget me."

"Oh, sorry, Judge. Monty Joe and Bobby Gray, take off your hats and shake Judge Hawkins's hand."

The brothers wiped off their hands, removed their hats, and shook hands all around.

Bobby Gray stared at his feet. "Monty Joe told me you were up here for some round-day-voo, Charlie." He glared at his brother. "Might have known better than to jump to conclusions."

"Conclusions? Jim said you were mighty *cozy* up here."

She couldn't believe Monty Joe thought that was an excuse for behaving like an idiot. Typical. "By cozy, I'm sure he meant warm and comfortable."

"What about that kiss we interrupted?"

Charlie wished she could disappear. Not only had her brothers totally humiliated her, but they had to remind her about how much she was like them in the idiocy department.

"Let's all go in and have a sandwich," suggested Ellen.

"No," insisted Charlie. "You were going to have a rehearsal dinner, and the arrival of my family lunatics shouldn't change anything. I'll stay here and make sure they crawl back under their rocks."

"I'll stay, too." Davis put his arm around Charlie's shoulder, making her feel a lot steadier on her feet. "Go on, Mom and Jim. I can take care of this."

"I wouldn't miss it for the world," said Ellen merrily. "Besides, I haven't been properly introduced to Charlie's brothers. After all, we'll soon be related."

"Related?" Monty Joe's eyes widened. Turning, he narrowed his eyes at Davis.

"You know, Jim, I think Charlie's going to be an interesting addition to our family," Ellen said musingly. "Think how lively family reunions will be."

Bobby Gray overheard her. "Addition to your family?"

Ellen nodded. "Of course. My baby boy and your little sister are getting married this fall. Didn't Charlie tell you?"

All eyes turned on Charlie. Silence. Total silence. She cleared her throat. Finally, she shot a desperate look at Davis, who understood all too well why she hadn't told her brothers about their faux engagement.

"I guess that's my fault," said Davis. "I only asked her last week and haven't given her much chance to think. Fact is, I'd planned to ask for your blessings next week, once Mom and Jim were on their way to Tokyo."

Bobby Gray turned hurt eyes on Charlie. "You're getting married and didn't call and tell us right away?"

"I'm sorry. But that still doesn't excuse the behavior of either of you." She did feel bad about hurting their feelings, but her overriding emotion was anger that they'd butt into her life this way. How could they? "Hasn't anything I've said for the past three years sunk into your heads? I'm not an eight-year-old motherless little girl anymore. I'm grown and I make my own decisions."

She blew out her bangs. "Please, Ellen. I'm so embarrassed about interrupting your rehearsal this way. Go to dinner and let me talk with my brothers."

"Charlie, I know you feel bad, but honestly, it doesn't matter," said Ellen gently. "In fact, it makes me care for you even more. And it certainly gives me hope that you're a match for my son. Until now, I couldn't help but worry that he'd run all over you."

"I should have warned you that your brothers were on their way," added Jim. "It completely slipped my mind."

"Now, here's what we're going to do," Ellen went on in a voice that allowed no argument. "We're going inside and getting cleaned up. Charlie, stop twisting your hands together. This is family, and no one thinks worse of you."

When everyone stood there in stunned silence, Ellen added, "Did you hear me? Move it."

The group moved as one, tripping over each other to get into the house. Charlie ran to her room, certain that she'd never be able to leave it. She sank, face first, down on her bed. If she hid in here until the wedding itself, maybe, just maybe, she could live through this weekend.

Her brothers had always been interfering and overprotective, and it had taken all of her strength to break away from them. She thought she'd managed to escape them by moving to Dallas. Her freedom had been merely a pretense on their part, though, based on their behavior the first time she ventured out of her shell. Her relationship with them, her freedom, was just as phony as her engagement to Davis.

And Davis. What was she going to do about him? Previously she'd been able to blame her reactions to him on the situation. This time, however, there'd been no such extenuating circumstances. She'd kissed him without hesitation.

The man was no better than her brothers. That's what happened when dealing with cowboy types. They were all the same.

She knew that with every inch of her being. She knew better than to become emotionally involved with this type, yet here she was, eager to be back in his company.

She threw her hands over her face. She had to stop this. Their engagement was only temporary. They didn't have a relationship. The whole thing was a farce.

The only answer had to be loneliness. Somehow,

when she was with Davis, she didn't feel lonely or isolated any more. He laughed at her jokes, and he seemed to understand how she felt, often before she did. When their eyes met across the room, they communicated without speaking a word.

It was like a glimpse of nirvana, but it wasn't real. That hurt the most.

It wasn't real.

Was she so needy that even a pretense would do since the reality wasn't available? That feigned intimacy would substitute for the real thing? Had she sunk so low, become that desperate?

Was she willing to give herself to Davis just to keep the wolves of loneliness at bay? The man didn't love her, that much was clear. Moreover she'd sworn she could never love a man like him, a cowboy in the making. And if it wasn't love, what kind of person did that make her?

What she wanted most was to escape, not her brothers, but herself, her own thoughts. Yet there was no getting away from who and what she was— a lonely woman with no hope, no end in sight. No wonder Joanne had been worried about leaving her.

Charlie had shut herself away so completely, had hidden her fears so well, that until now she hadn't admitted their existence. But taking that small step had been the forewarning that the walls she'd built would soon come tumbling down. They'd been constructed on such weak foundations, they didn't stand a chance.

Now she was faced with a choice. There was no going back. She could either change, or end up exactly what she was now: a woman so alone, so isolated, that she was willing to do nearly anything to keep from facing herself.

No. She hadn't sunk that low. And she wouldn't. Charlie found her backbone, her strength, buried somewhere under that needy little girl. She pushed herself off the bed. Going into the bathroom, she ran icy cold water over her face until it stung.

It was time to snap out of it. No more hiding, no more feeling inadequate. Enough. She'd face the group out there with bravery, if little else.

Feeling as though she was about to face a firing squad, she entered the living room. But no one noticed her. They were all laughing, sides heaving, patting their thighs, and Ellen had tears streaming down her face.

Charlie laughed at herself. She'd been so self-centered, she was sure the whole gang of them would be talking about her. Instead they were having a great time—without her. She stood on the outskirts, watching, wondering if she should go back to her room, but then Ellen saw her.

"Charlie, you just missed my story about the first time Jim proposed to me."

Her gaze shot to Jim. He had a self-satisfied smile on his face: the man who'd gotten what he'd set out to get. "I'm sorry I missed it."

Jim stood. "It's time to get this show on the road. We've decided to take Monty Joe's truck to the restaurant. Ellen's never ridden in the back of a pickup, and she's insistent."

Ellen grinned. "It looks like this is my lucky week." She gazed into Jim's eyes. "All my wishes are being granted."

Charlie's chest heaved, making her hiccough. She folded her arms around herself. If only *one* of her wishes would be granted.

An odd noise awoke Charlie from a deep sleep. Leaning up on her elbow, she listened closely. Nothing. In a strange house, any sound might seem peculiar. Laying her head back on the pillow, she closed her eyes, then bolted upright.

There was the clamor again, like the sound of a door opening and closing and opening again.

Next she heard whispers—her brothers' whispers.

Tossing off the bedcovers, she bounced from the bed and dashed to her bedroom door. The room was nearly pitch black, and it took a moment for her to find the doorknob. When she threw open the door, though, the noise stopped.

A faint light coming from her brothers' room

dimmed as the door quickly closed. She headed down the hall and yanked their door open.

Monty Joe's voice filled the hallway. "I told you your snoring would wake her, Bobby Gray."

"Are you guys trying to drive me mad?" she whispered. "What the dickens were you doing out in the hall?"

"Consider us your guardian angels."

"What were you doing, standing guard?" When she said it, she hadn't believed it, but the look on their faces said that's exactly what they'd been up to.

"Told you the tag-team was a bad idea," said Bobby Gray.

"Shh. Keep your voices down. You've embarrassed me enough already." How could they do this to her? Her sleepy eyes narrowed. "What makes you think I need—or want—a guard?"

"We're just making sure you get your rest, so to speak," replied Bobby Gray.

Just then, they turned at the sound of a door opening down the hall. Charlie recognized Davis in spite of the lack of light.

As he felt his way down the hall, she asked her brothers, "What, besides the two of you, could possibly disturb me?"

The brothers looked at Davis. Davis smiled. "I think watching out for her was a great idea."

Monty Joe clapped him on the back. "I hoped you'd see it that way."

There followed much backslapping and general bonding between the men. Charlie wondered if she was still sleeping. She pinched herself—nope.

Here Davis was, proving he was just as much an idiot as any cowboy she'd ever met. "What do you mean, Davis, that it was a great idea? Don't you realize they don't trust either of us?"

She crossed her arms in front of her. "Monty Joe and Bobby Gray, if you don't get into your pickup this minute and head back to the ranch, I'm never speaking to you again."

She turned to go.

Davis spoke up. "I feel a lot better, Charlie, knowing you've got brothers like this to look out for your best interests."

Maybe her brothers weren't so bad after all. At least *they* were motivated by love for her when they acted like buffoons. But what was Davis's excuse?

"Grab your bathrobe, Charlie, and come out to the kitchen," ordered Monty Joe. "I'll make you some hot chocolate like I used to when you were a kid and had bad dreams. Otherwise, you'll never go back to sleep."

Charlie sighed. He was right—she wouldn't be able to sleep now. It was sweet of him to remember about the hot chocolate. "I don't have a robe," she mumbled, more for the sake of not going along with everything he said, than any other reason.

"This should keep you warm." Davis removed his pajama shirt and wrapped it around her shoulders. Charlie could just imagine the smirks on her brothers' faces. "Mind if I join you for that hot chocolate?"

"Yes," replied Charlie.

At the same moment, both Monty Joe and Bobby Gray said, "No."

"In for a penny," mumbled Charlie. "The more the merrier."

As the group stumbled down the hall, she cringed at every sound they made. All she needed now was to have the entire house in an uproar because of her. When they came down the stairs, they saw a light already on in the kitchen.

Ellen stood in the doorway with empty mugs in her hands. "Just in time, children. I've got milk heating on the stove."

Good heavens, had she heard every word? "I'm sorry we woke you, Ellen."

"You didn't." She laughed. "I'm so excited about the wedding, I simply couldn't sleep. When I heard you were coming for hot chocolate, I thought it was something I could do rather than tossing and turning."

Once Monty Joe caught sight of Charlie in the

light, he immediately came over and made a move to button Davis's shirt to hide her pajamas.

"Just stop it, already," she said irritably as she shook herself free.

Monty Joe turned to Davis. "She's kind of cranky when she's woken from a deep sleep."

"I can see that."

"She's always mean as a sow in the mornings," added Bobby Gray.

Davis coughed, fighting back a laugh. "That's good to know."

He wanted to know details like this about Charlie. All the little stuff you don't know about someone until you've known them for years. "What was she like as a kid?"

"Stubborn as a mule. She wasn't scared of anything," replied Monty Joe as he turned a kitchen chair around and took a seat on it, leaning his head on the chair's back. "I'll never forget the time she decided to ride Diablo."

Bobby Gray guffawed. "Diablo won't let us forget it, either."

As Ellen poured the steaming hot chocolate into mugs and began handing them out, the brothers continued their story. Davis took a chair beside Charlie, who snarled at him, then quickly buried her face in her hands. Davis grinned.

Her brothers both had the same single dimple as Charlie. It had to be a dominant gene.

"She was only eight years old, and Diablo was pretty wild. Our stable foreman hadn't had much luck with him, and even I was thrown. But Charlie was certain Diablo would let her ride him."

Davis imagined Charlie as a tow-headed tot. She must have been the apple of her protective brothers' eyes. He could almost picture how much fun it would be to have kids who looked like her, demanding horsie rides on his knees. Davis bit his tongue. What has he thinking? Him? Kids?

"So early one morning, she snuck out of the house, led the horse to the field. When Diablo tried to act up, she stuck a handful of carrots into the crazed animal's mouth. And dang if the horse didn't calm down and let her mount him—bareback."

Bobby Gray hopped onto the counter near where Ellen stood. "Yeah, but the problem is, now he won't take a rider until he's been fed his carrots."

"And he's the best saddle horse on the Nelson Ranch," commented Charlie from between her fingers.

Like a signal, Davis snapped his fingers. He had to be the slowest man on earth not to have known before now. He'd even seen photographs of the famous brothers, who resembled each other enough to be identical twins. If their coloring had been the same, it would be next to impossible to tell them apart.

Curly-haired like their sister, they exuded a rugged male confidence. Considering the number of women who thought the brothers had been sent down from heaven for womankind's enjoyment, Davis found it interesting that neither had ever married. "I never made the connection. I can't believe that when I heard your names, I didn't make the connection. You guys are Monty Joe and Bobby Gray Nelson of the Nelson Ranch!"

"All the wedding excitement probably caused your memory lapse," mumbled Charlie. "I'm sure I must have mentioned it."

"Not even once. Not even when you were telling me how you felt about cowboys." This explained exactly why she didn't want to fall in love with one. What man could live up to the Nelson brothers, who had been famous on the rodeo circuit for years? Their fame had grown thanks to the cattle produced by the Nelson Ranch. They were the livestock providers to one of the largest rodeos in the country.

And they were Charlie's brothers.

Davis didn't stand a chance when measured next to them.

Ellen handed him his mug. He took a scalding sip.

"Now that you mention the ranch, Bobby Gray, that reminds me." Ellen took a seat across from Charlie. "I'm so excited—Charlie's brothers have decided to give an engagement party . . ."

Monty Joe interrupted, "Not a prissy engagement party—we're giving an engagement *barbecue* . . ."

Ellen continued, "Next weekend, so there'll be time . . ."

"We already called and invited a few of our cousins . . ."

"For Jim and me to attend before . . ."

"Aunt Irabelle assured me that cousins Jimmy, Ricky, and Jerry will come . . ."

Bobby Gray spoke up, "Yeah, and Uncle Bob said he and his kids wouldn't miss it for the world . . ."

" . . . we have to leave for Tokyo!" his mother finished.

Dead silence greeted her.

Ellen looked at Charlie, and then at Davis. "Isn't this wonderful?"

"Just peachy," muttered Charlie, her expression hidden by her coffee mug.

"It's a terrific idea." Davis scratched his chin, playing for time. "Did you run it past Jim?"

"Oh, that wasn't necessary," Ellen replied.

"It wasn't?"

"I think it's time to finish your chocolate and go back to bed. Looks like Charlie is half-asleep." Ellen patted Davis on the shoulder. "And I didn't need to mention the barbecue to Jim. It was *his* idea."

Chapter Ten

"I should be giving you the silent treatment," said Charlie as she baited Davis's hook the next morning.

He ignored her. For a moment, she considered using *him* as bait instead. She swung her bare feet over the pier and cautiously dipped her toe into the water. Too cold. Pulling her feet up under her, she added, "First, you turn me into a phony."

Davis, who sat directly beside her, stiffened but didn't utter a word. The coward was afraid to face her.

"Then, instead of the 'one measly night' you promised, it turns into a weekend and a wedding." Charlie's hands shook but she managed to get the minnow on the line.

137

"And now this, Davis Murphy, is the topper. You've involved my whole entire family. You've involved cousins I haven't seen since my parents' funeral!"

"You're not the only one upset over what's been going on." His face muscles twitched. "I wanted to wallop Jim when I saw him this morning. It's a good thing he's leaving the country next week."

"Yeah, of course you'd think violence would be the answer."

"I didn't touch him. And there's my mother, who's elated over you joining our family. She's in there now, bonding with your brothers, because she thinks that now she's getting not only a daughter in this deal, but also two additional sons." Davis swung his line out into the water. "I think I know how to fix it all."

"You do?"

He nodded and finally turned her way. His eyes were bloodshot. In fact, his whole face looked wan. Had he slept at all last night? She resisted an urge to tuck him back in bed. The man deserved to suffer for what he'd put her through.

"You can tell your brothers we broke up this morning. It's not too late·to cancel the barbecue."

"What a terrific idea," she said sarcastically. "I do so want to see your innards strewn on the highway between here and south Texas."

"Do you have any better ideas?"

"No." Charlie couldn't think of anything. Perhaps that was the problem. Ever since she'd agreed to Davis's little plan, she hadn't been able to think. "Maybe we should just go through with the barbecue, and then, in a few weeks when things have calmed down, I can write them a note saying I met another man."

"And when they demand to meet him?"

He had a point. It would involve more lies and she'd prevaricated more than enough to last her a lifetime. At some time her brothers would figure it out. Monty Joe was a lot more perceptive than he appeared to be.

Charlie pulled up her knees and rested her chin on them. What was she going to do?

Davis ran his thumb down her cheek. He swallowed, hard, and she saw his Adam's apple bob. "In that case, Charlie, this whole engagement thing isn't so bad."

Her whole body silenced, stilled, like an animal frozen in headlights.

"I mean, if I have to be engaged to someone, I'm glad it's you. I've been a fan of the Nelson brothers for most of my life. I've watched them compete. If I have to get married someday—and I don't want to rush this—I could do a lot worse than marry into your family. So what do you say?"

No. No. She'd always dreamed of the day she'd have handsome men proposing to her. That day seemed to have arrived. In her fantasy, she was vivacious, beautiful and flirtatious, with men writing poems about her eyes. Instead, she got Philip asking her to marry him because she'd broken up with him. Now Davis was proposing—to marry her brothers. Could life get any worse?

She suspected it could. Some remote part of her, some hidden voice, had leaped with joy at the thought of marrying Davis. That was before she'd realized he didn't want *her*. She was a woman he could never find acceptable, a woman who could please his mother, but never him.

"How nice that you approve of my family." She wouldn't let him know how he'd hurt her. That would sting even more. "The only problem is—how I feel about you."

She pushed away from him and ran to the house, before he could spot her tears. She'd see this thing through, and then she'd make a point of never again becoming entangled with another cowboy.

"Stop fidgeting," insisted Davis as he pinned the boutonniere on Jim. Using his hip, he slammed the refrigerator shut, where the flowers had been stored to keep them fresh.

"I wouldn't need to fidget if you'd quit fussing over me like a hen," replied Jim dryly.

"The way I see it, you're lucky you're getting the chicken treatment instead of what I'd like to do." Davis smoothed Jim's lapel, then stepped back. "Mom wouldn't want you to come to the altar bruised."

"What fly is up your coattails, now?"

"Like you don't know." Perhaps one little sucker punch? "Mom told me that *you'd* suggested the barbecue."

"Well, son, at the rate you and Charlie are going, I figured you could use all the help you can get."

"You've involved her family, Jim. It's not right. Charlie's been a real sport helping me out, and now you've put her in a terrible position."

Jim laughed and slapped his thigh. "Yee-gads, the two of you are stubborn. You belong together. Otherwise, I'd have put a stop to this thing from the get-go."

"Getting married has addled your brain, Jim."

"Don't be a horse's backside. You belong with Charlie just as surely as I belong with your mom, and it's clear as glass to anyone who watches you together."

"Charlie sure doesn't feel that way. She won't have me." One thing he knew. Somehow he'd hurt her. Davis wasn't sure how, but he'd hurt her just as surely as if he'd punched *her* in the gut. Why couldn't he have kept his stupid mouth shut?

"What makes you so sure she won't have you?"

"I asked her." She didn't want to marry him, which wasn't surprising. He'd never be able to live up to her brothers' image. But he hoped she at least found him tolerable; heaven knew, she was the most tolerable woman he'd ever met. And now he'd gone and hurt her.

She didn't want him to break the engagement, but she'd made it clear she had no intention of it continuing a moment longer than necessary. He only wished it didn't make him feel so funny, like his insides were heavy.

His mother's worries may have been accurate. With her and Jim leaving, who would he have to talk to or be himself around? He felt lonely already, and they hadn't even left. He'd never realized that he'd miss Charlie, who would leave his life as well. Until now.

And it made him feel strange. Like he was losing his best friend.

"If Charlie turned you down, then you screwed up the question." Jim threw up his hands. "Do I have to spell things out for you? Did you tell her how you feel?"

"You don't understand, Jim. How can I tell a

woman that I'm so hungry for her company that I ache inside?"

"You tell her that you love her, that's how."

"Love?" Davis was incredulous. "Have you lost your mind?"

"Stubborn, stubborn, stubborn. Just like your mother." Jim looked at the wall clock. "We're due outside now. Have you got the ring?"

Davis patted his coat pocket. No ring. He stuck his hands in his pants, only to come up empty. His heart pounded. "Shoot, I think I lost it."

Jim rolled his eyes. "Check your inside left breast pocket."

Davis smiled sheepishly when he pulled the ring out. "Got it."

"Good. I only hope you got what I was trying to tell you, too. Let's go."

Within minutes, he and Jim were standing on the gaily decorated gazebo, watching Charlie walk down the pier, followed by Ellen. Elvis's song *"I Can't Help Falling in Love with You"* played over strategically placed stereo speakers.

His mom was a natural organizer. She'd managed to rope in Charlie's brothers, who had good-naturedly acted as ushers. Monty Joe let out a cat-call when he caught sight of Ellen, who looked beautiful and excited in her youthful winter white suit. Everyone laughed, and Davis heard his Uncle Roy comment about what a lucky man Jim was.

The music contributed to the festive mood. Jim and Ellen's radiant joy was infectious, and the wedding guests were jubilant. Like Davis, they'd waited a long time to see the couple who so obviously loved each other make a commitment.

Davis scratched an itch on his hand, idling wondering if he'd been bitten by an insect.

"Wise men say . . ." sang Elvis.

As Charlie approached, Davis saw she was pale, her smile forced. She'd avoided him all day, and it was apparent she still hurt from their earlier conversation. If he could, he'd take back the day, take back whatever he'd said that gave her pain.

He tried to meet her eye. She looked anywhere, everywhere, but at him, as if in her mind he no longer existed. Which was what he deserved for causing her distress.

He scratched another spot on his neck. Darn mosquitos.

There had to be a way to make it up to her. To make her dimple reappear. To make her face light up in laughter. If only he knew how to fix things.

Elvis crooned on.

Ellen smiled warmly at Davis as she took her place beside Jim, her happiness nearly bringing Davis to his knees. Is that what it meant to know you loved someone and their love was returned?

His whole face began to itch. A whole herd of mosquitos must have turned out for the wedding.

Again, he glanced at Charlie. She was so pretty in blue, like a spring flower blooming after a long brown winter. She deserved the best that life had to offer. She deserved a man who'd adore her, who'd make her proud.

He'd find a way to fix things for her, and maybe, on the flight back to Dallas, he'd find a way to make up for having hurt her. Just then, Charlie met his gaze. Finally. She gave him a small smile and a flicker of hope flamed in his chest. Somehow, he'd find a way.

"Falling in love . . ."

Chapter Eleven

"I don't need that horse salve, Lily," said Davis as he examined his face in the small mirror he held. "It's been three days. Surely the hives are starting to fade."

"Yeah, those blotches are part of your normal complexion," replied Lily as she prepared to apply the ointment on Davis's face. "Now sit still so I can fix you up."

Davis laid the mirror on his desk, then let out a long-suffering sigh. If he didn't let her have her way with him, he'd never hear the end of it.

"You look like a survivor of a swarm of locusts."

"Very funny." Davis sat still as she rubbed the smelly goo on his face. "It's just that weddings give me hives."

Lily rolled her eyes. "I only hope engagement barbecues don't, because your reputation may not survive another bout."

"The doctor assured me they'll go away."

"Did he mention scarring?"

"Are you done yet?"

"I'm finished with the ointment." Lily screwed the lid back on the jar, then ostentatiously placed it directly on the desk in front of him. "However, I'm not sure I'm done giving you a hard time."

Davis made a face at her. "I've got work to do, even if you don't."

"All right, already." Lily walked toward the door. "But I'll be back."

Davis growled, thinking she had a lot in common with Schwarzenegger. He pulled out a rope and looped it into a lasso, then took careful aim at the hitching post located in a corner of his office. Other executives had installed miniature putting greens so they could practice their golf putts. He'd figured if he was forced to work on contracts, at least he'd be able to get in a little roping when his soul cried out for the prairie.

And his soul was crying out right now . . . but for something else, or rather someone else. Charlie.

She'd refused to fly back to Dallas with him. Instead, she'd ridden back with her brothers. Which hadn't been such a bad thing, since Davis had looked so ridiculous with red welts all over him.

But he missed her.

When Lily had interrupted him to apply the ointment, he'd been looking through his address book—his little black book. Trying unsuccessfully to find a woman he felt like calling. Davis tossed the lasso toward the post. He overthrew and the rope slapped against the wall.

Davis sat up straight. He hadn't missed that post even once in the past year and a half. What was he doing, sitting here mooning over Charlie, when he could be phoning some woman to comfort his weary soul? He glanced at the name, Avis, wondering if he should call her. She always did try harder. But what was the use? Davis ripped the "A" page from his address book and tore it into shreds.

He tossed the lasso again. Perfect. That proved he could still concentrate. Charlie hadn't *totally* destroyed his ability to focus.

With a quick flip of the wrist, he freed the lasso and pulled it back to him. Looping it again, he threw once more. Another miss.

Davis grabbed the "B" page from the book, wadded it up and threw it across the room. There was only one woman who'd be able to make him feel any better, and she wouldn't return his calls.

He'd left two messages for her at work and three at home. Why wouldn't Charlie talk with him? Surely, if they talked, they could iron things out.

Davis carefully aimed his lasso at the hitching post. Another miss. The "C" page went the way of the first two. What was the point? There wasn't another woman for him. There was only Charlie.

At some point she'd *have* to talk with him, since they were expected at the Nelson Ranch on Saturday. Maybe he was going about this the wrong way? Two could play hard to get.

It was already Wednesday. Before long, she'd have to call him if she didn't want her brothers to send out a posse. Davis smiled.

Once they were on their way to Houston, he'd be able to find out how he'd hurt her feelings. He'd even follow Jim's advice, if that would repair things between them. Davis simply needed to use a little more finesse, a little more charm and a few more kisses. Charlie would soon be singing a different tune.

Davis tore all the pages from his little black book and threw the whole thing into the wastebasket. This time, when he aimed the lasso, it slipped perfectly into place around the hitching post.

He took it as a sign that his plans were perfect, too.

* * *

Davis shifted uncomfortably in the passenger seat of Charlie's car. They'd been driving more than four hours. They had to be nearing the Nelson Ranch soon. She sure didn't drive like any librarian he'd ever heard of, unless no one had bothered telling him that the word librarian was synonymous with speed demon.

When she'd finally broken down and called him, she insisted that she drive. No matter how many arguments he'd come up with for flying, she'd dug in her heels. *She* would drive.

He thought perhaps that would work to his advantage. But so far, things had fizzled. Charlie was concentrating too hard on her driving to be charmed, and he couldn't exactly ask her to practice kissing. Davis sighed.

He didn't have much time left. There had to be some way to convince her that marrying him was a good choice.

"Charlie, I know I can't live up to the image of your brothers. No man could."

She shrugged. "They're nice guys but they aren't exactly my ideals."

"Aren't they the reason why you won't become involved with a cowboy?"

Charlie gripped the steering wheel with white knuckles. "No."

Just because she answered in a monosyllable

didn't mean she was telling him the truth. He'd heard enough women say no and then turn around and say yes.

"I'm just starting out, but I've got a successful track record behind me of doing what I've said I'd do."

No answer to that one.

"In this day and age, very few people could afford a huge spread like the Nelson Ranch starting out. One day, if my plans work out, I'm hoping to be able to talk about my place with similar pride."

Obviously this wasn't working. He needed another way to get her talking. It was his only hope of figuring out how to convince her to marry him. "How about you?"

She didn't say anything for a moment as she slowed and made a turn onto a smaller highway. "Me?"

"Yes. What do you, Charlie Nelson, want in life? What are you looking for in a mate? Do you have any plans?"

"I like working at the library. I'd like to become a library director at some point."

"That's it?"

She looked at him from the corner of her eyes. "Pretty much covers it."

"Don't you want to get married someday?"

"Most women do, and I'm like most women in that. I just haven't found the right man."

Davis liked to think she had. Nothing she said encouraged him. "So what is your Mr. Right like?"

"I'd like him to be able to make me laugh."

He had that covered.

"He'd have to be intelligent . . ."

So far so good. He might not be brilliant, but he was pretty quick on his feet.

"But he shouldn't be boring, either."

She must be talking about that egghead, Philip. Davis was certain that he, himself, was anything but boring.

"I'd like him to be good-looking, but not so good-looking that I'd have to worry about him around other women."

Was she picking on him about his face? The hives had almost faded entirely, but there were still traces. "If you love each other, that shouldn't matter, should it?"

"I guess not. I think he should be successful, but I don't measure that in money, but in a sense of achievement and pursuing his interests. And he should be a nice guy, someone I could trust."

Better and better. Davis was a perfect fit. He opened his mouth to tell her, but she spoke before he had a chance.

"And most importantly, he won't be a cowboy.

He won't be interested in anything remotely connected with cows, ranches or rodeos."

That was the nail in his coffin. And if it wasn't because of her brothers, then why was it? "What's wrong with cowboys?"

"Probably everything that appeals to you about becoming one, Davis."

Charlie turned down a two-lane road. "Cowboys are risk-takers, and they don't always use their heads in determining when they should act. They're loners by nature and always have to be heroes, chasing after buckles, chasing after the emotional highs, chasing after some dream of the Old West and independence."

Davis rubbed his forehead. He heard what she said, but he didn't understand why this was a problem.

"I'm not saying it's wrong, Davis. I'm just saying it's not how I want to spend *my* life. I made a conscious decision to leave the ranch three long years ago, and I have no intention of coming back again except for quick visits. My share of this place gets plowed back into it for improvements. I live off my income as a librarian. This is my brothers' dream, and maybe your dream, but it's not mine."

"Okay. I think I can understand that, but what is *your* dream?"

"A man who works a nine-to-five job and comes

home to me. Kids. Church and Sunday school. Volunteering for the PTA. Occasional travel. A nice little brick house with three bedrooms and two baths and a reasonable mortgage."

Charlie turned into the ranch. Overhead, suspended between two metal posts, was a white painted wrought-iron sign proclaiming *The Nelson Ranch*.

"My dream isn't very exciting," she continued, "but it's mine."

It was plenty exciting—too bad it depressed him. He turned his concentration to their surroundings and looked around with interest. In the distance he could see a windmill and a couple of L-shaped cattle sheds beside a pond and what looked like watering troughs. His interest peaked. He couldn't see the main house yet or even the bunkhouse.

There had to be room for him in her future. "It's a very nice dream, Charlie. It's almost identical to mine, and I can't understand why it excludes a husband who's a cowboy."

When she started to deny how similar their dreams were, he added, "It's your dream, I accept that. I'd just like to know why a guy like me couldn't share it. What makes you so certain?"

"Don't be ludicrous," She glared at him. "You'd be bored within a day of playing house. You'd be out there looking for another risk so you'd feel alive rather than buried in parenthood and the ties of matrimony and monogamy."

As they came over a small crest, Davis saw the main ranch for the first time. It had a red tile roof, stucco walls and southwestern flair. It was a large, sprawling building, obviously added onto over the years as the ranch grew.

Davis chewed over what Charlie had said. "So you think a cowboy is incapable of monogamy and being happily married?"

"That's not what I'm saying."

"That's *exactly* what you said, Charlie." How could he ever be bored with a woman like her by his side? One moment prissy as all get out, up on her high horse, and the next scrunching up her nose and doing something utterly outrageous. And, most surprising of all, she was more appealing than any woman he'd ever met. No, he'd never feel tied down or bored with her.

Charlie turned down a long paved driveway leading to the rear of the house, where a large garage had been built. She stopped the car just to the left of the house. To the rear of the building, Davis saw a covered patio and a pool area already decorated for the barbecue. The smell of burning mesquite was heavy in the air, as well as barbecuing beef and ham.

Charlie was wrong. She'd discounted something

important—love didn't make distinctions about career choices.

It hit Davis that no matter how much he denied it to himself, Jim was right. He loved Charlie with all his heart.

Davis had been stubbornly denying the truth about his feelings for her. He wasn't sure when or how it happened, but now that he looked into his heart, he knew he'd never be the same again. Nothing but a lifelong commitment would be enough; that was what made life possible. Love had all the answers.

He needed her by his side. For some reason, she refused to allow herself to need him. "So your beliefs about cowboys are why you didn't take me seriously when I suggested we get married?"

Charlie laughed, the sound coming from low in her throat. "You were proposing to the Nelson brothers, not me." She swung open her door to greet her brothers, who were rushing to the car.

What did she mean by that? Perhaps Jim was right—he'd screwed up the question. He'd try again as soon as he got a moment alone with her. While he'd heard of other people being in love with someone who didn't return their love, he was sure that wasn't the case between him and Charlie.

He watched her trade hugs with her brothers with a smile on her face, yet there was a tightness about her brow that suggested she was troubled. Like him. While she denied it intellectually, every indication led him to believe she cared for him as much as he cared for her.

Jim had accused *him* of being stubborn, but Davis suspected that Charlie won the prize. Climbing out of the car, he stretched his legs, then shook hands with Monty Joe and Bobby Gray.

"Already letting her take you for a drive, huh, Davis?" asked Bobby Gray. "It must be true love."

Davis laughed. "You know how she is. She decided she wanted to drive. Unless I'd rendered her unconscious, I didn't see any other way to change her mind."

Charlie slapped his arm playfully. "Nonsense. I knew my way here and you didn't. Besides, I let you fly us to the lake."

"Well, come on in and let us show you around," said Monty Joe. "We've got a few hours before the party starts, if you'd like a short tour of the ranch."

Davis grinned from ear to ear. Talk about a dream come true. He'd read everything he could about the Nelson brothers and their famous ranch, but to actually get to see it in person was amazing. Almost like Christmas morning when he was a kid and found a few surprises under the tree that he hadn't known he wanted. Wishes he had never known could come true.

"Go have fun," said Charlie. "Don't forget to have him back in time, Monty Joe."

She turned to Davis. "I think Jim said he and Ellen would arrive in about an hour, so I'll stick around here to welcome them."

"Thanks." Davis leaned over and gave her a quick kiss. Her eyes widened.

Evidently Bobby Gray noticed that Davis was tempted to give her a longer embrace, because he grabbed Davis's arm. "There'll be time enough for that later. If we want to have you back for the barbecue, we need to head out now."

Davis stepped back from Charlie. "See you later."

"You bet," she replied with a relieved smile.

He should have figured out some way to kiss her before now. It might have helped his case.

Charlie wanted to fan her cheeks. How could one swift kiss from Davis make her feel this way? Better hurry him on his way before she grabbed him and refused to let go. "Monty Joe, don't use up all the time showing him your latest equipment. Take him to see the bunkhouse and make sure he gets to see one of the cattle sheds."

"Yes'm," replied her brother with a sheepish grin.

She'd been kidding him for years over the visitor who'd come and never seen the ranch. Instead, he'd spent the whole visit with her brothers in the equipment buildings, each the size of a football field, looking at tractors and semi-trailers. "He'd probably like to meet the vet and the foreman, too."

Monty Joe laughed. "We'd better get out of here before she gives us an itinerary."

Charlie waved as they drove off in the four-wheeler, feeling a little deserted even though she'd been the one insisting they go.

Turning toward the house, she saw the family dogs dart toward her. "Ali and Ray! Good dogs. You're glad to see me, aren't you?"

She'd helped bottle-feed the collies seven years earlier when their mother had died. A neighbor had offered the pups to the Nelson kids since he didn't want to be saddled with the responsibility of taking care of such young puppies. They'd been the perfect addition to the Nelson family, and had ruled the ranch ever since.

Charlie hugged them closely and buried her face in their thick white fur. One of the ranch hands took care of bathing them, and they smelled of saddle soap. She hadn't realized how much she'd missed them. With Joanne moving out soon, there was no reason why she couldn't get a dog of her own, even if Ali and Ray were irreplaceable in her heart.

She grinned, picked up her suitcase and headed inside. She'd definitely get a collie of her own. It would be impossible to feel lonely when she had 70 pounds of dog sitting on her chest.

* * *

There was nothing, thought Charlie, like a barbecue grilled on the Nelson Ranch. Their cook, Sing Hop, had a special sauce he prepared unlike anything she'd tasted elsewhere. It was just spicy enough to leave a tang in her mouth, yet not so hot that steam shot out of her ears.

She and Davis had been toasted by her brothers, aunts and uncles, Jim and Ellen, neighbors, relatives and kissing cousins by the score. The lemonade and iced tea flowed like a Texas stream.

Tables had been set up near the pool area, and the house was open to show off the treasures of the ranch. Overhead several yellow-and-white-striped awnings had been erected. The early March weather had cooperated as well. A light breeze stirred the air, but it was warm enough to go without a sweater. And although the sun had already gone down for the day, the area was well-lit with Tiki lanterns and outdoor spotlights.

Davis, seated beside her, had thoroughly enjoyed his tour of the ranch and kept spouting off statistics about the size of it. She'd grown up knowing the ranch was just over thirty-five square miles and composed of more than 30,000 acres, but it was all new to Davis. Although she'd never admit it, she did feel a certain pride in having been a part of the ranch. Knowing the history of her roots helped her feel more grounded and self-assured.

Monty Joe stood and yelled for everyone's attention.

Charlie grinned and sat up straight, certain he'd find another way to toast her upcoming nuptials, and wondering if he'd work a naughty pun into it. The guys had been trying to one-up each other all evening.

"As most of you know," said Monty Joe, "we supply the local rodeo with its stock for their yearly competition. It kicks off tomorrow, and we have a little surprise in store for you."

The sound of applause filled the air as well as a few wolf whistles. "Bobby Gray and I agreed to give an exhibition performance this year, and we're pleased to say there'll be another addition to the Nelson contingent."

The guests clapped even louder, and a few heads turned to look her way. Charlie hadn't ridden in years, and there was no way she could be talked into it now, even if Monty Joe thought he could convince her through public humiliation. She shook her head. He knew she didn't stand a chance without having practiced.

Then she felt rather than saw Davis grin. Turning, she watched him stand, as if in slow motion. "Not only am I proud to become a part of this great family, but I'm ready and willing to join it in the arena."

"That's right, folks. Davis is going to compete in the steer roping event. We hope you'll all be there to cheer him on."

Now their guests applauded even louder than before. Whistling and cheers filled the air, but Charlie hardly heard the cacophony. She couldn't believe it. Even though Davis had told her he'd trained for the rodeo, and steer roping in particular, that didn't make it safe. How could her brothers do this? And why would Davis agree to something so foolish?

She literally shook with fury. By risking his neck, it proved to her how utterly unsuited they were for each other. How she felt about him didn't matter; all that mattered were the risks he chose to take without giving her one thought.

He could have discussed it with her first. Her brothers could have brought it up to her before asking him. This was so typical of men, not bothering the little woman.

She might be small, but that didn't mean she wouldn't express her views on Davis's stupidity and her brother's idiotic behavior. As soon as the barbecue guests left, she'd set things straight.

Meanwhile, she did her best to smile and pretend she was having a good time.

Unfortunately, her brothers had set up a dance

floor, and the guests who'd finished eating had already begun a line dance. Everyone seemed to take it as a given that the bride-to-be and her intended would dance, too.

When the band struck up another song, Davis asked, "Shall we?"

Could she plead a headache? Monty Joe would never let her get away with it. "If we have to, but let's just dance one."

"What's wrong?" he asked as he led her onto the floor.

"Let's talk about it later." Just her luck—it was a slow dance, which involved being close, almost too close to Davis for her comfort. She kept as much distance between them as possible as he led them around the dance floor.

"Are you mad about something?"

"What could I possibly be mad about?" she spat out. He ought to know what was bothering her—she'd told him often enough.

"I don't know, but sure as shootin', you're mad."

"I can't believe you're going to compete tomorrow."

Davis grinned and pulled her closer as he swung her around. "Is that all? It's no big deal."

"That's where you're wrong—it's a *very* big deal. You could get yourself killed."

"I don't think that's very likely."

She stopped dancing. "It can and does happen. I've seen it."

Davis dragged her along for a step or two until she reluctantly followed his steps. "I could also be hit on the head by a meteor, but I'm willing to take my chances in order to stay outdoors snuggling with you."

"Very funny." There had to be some way to convince him that he shouldn't do this. What would she do if something happened to him?

"Don't do it, Davis. It would mean a lot to me if you didn't."

"You can't be serious."

She nodded.

Now Davis stopped dancing. He led her to a shadowy area just off the dance floor. "What is this all about?"

"You asked me earlier why a cowboy was out of the question for me. What you've got planned for tomorrow answers your question."

Davis rubbed his eyes. They felt gritty, as if they were full of sand. "So competing tomorrow would be taking a needless risk."

"My point exactly. Don't do it, Davis."

He had the feeling that if he backed down, she'd agree right here and now to marry him. But he'd dreamed and worked and planned for this moment for years. It was more than a childhood aspiration.

How could he make that clear to her, and yet retain any chance of a relationship between them?

"All my life, Charlie, I've been following some-one else's dreams and postponed my own. When my dad died . . ." Davis's voice broke. Even after all these years, talking about it still stung.

Charlie wrapped her arms around him, giving him strength in a way he couldn't explain. It encouraged him to believe there had to be a way to work things out.

"I've lived my father's dream of turning Murphy Title into a successful business. I've taken care of my responsibilities since I was an adolescent. I de-serve an opportunity to achieve at least one of *my* dreams, Charlie. I've worked too hard for this mo-ment. Please, don't ask me to give it up."

She let go of him. Even in the darkness, he could see tears filling her eyes. Reaching up to wipe them away, he lowered his hand when she stepped back.

"Charlie, I love you."

"I love you, too, Davis. But I just can't do this. I'm going home in the morning. There's no way on earth I can stand around and watch you get maimed or killed."

"And afterwards?"

"It's over, Davis. You're a cowboy, through and through. I can't afford to love you." She turned and walked over to join her brothers, who were standing near the dance floor.

Davis wanted to destroy something. He wanted to kick and beat and rip at something. But what was the point, when what he really wanted was to destroy the dream inside himself that Charlie couldn't love.

Chapter Twelve

Charlie placed her suitcase in the back seat of her car. The early morning chill clung heavily in the air, forcing a shiver from her body. Determinedly, she got into the car and headed for the bunkhouse to see the ranch foreman, Willie Fred Miller.

She needed to make arrangements for Davis to return to Dallas since she would be leaving him without a way back home. The bunkhouse was only two miles from the main house, and she arrived in only a few minutes.

She headed for the main barn, where she was certain she'd find Willie Fred. Sure enough, he was seated in his office going over paperwork. Charlie tapped on the door frame.

"Charlie, I wasn't expecting you this morning." He stood and offered her his hand.

She returned his friendly gesture. They didn't know each other that well, since he took the job at the ranch just after she'd left to go to Dallas. She'd never had a chance to get to know him, but he always welcomed her with a kind and gentle smile.

Davis's plans to compete in the rodeo brought things to the surface that she had carefully buried. How her parents had been killed in an auto accident while on their way to compete; how the previous ranch foreman, Hank Rowan, the man who'd placed her on the back of her first pony, had been killed while competing in the last rodeo she'd ever attended.

Charlie was heartsick at having people she loved taken away.

"I've had a change of plans, Willie Fred. I need to get home to Dallas this morning, and Davis will need transportation back later in the day. I wondered if you could make arrangements for him?"

"I'd be happy to help, Charlie. Are you sure there's nothing I can do to make it possible for you to stay? Your brothers will be mighty disappointed that you're leaving so soon."

"I know. But there's nothing to be done. I have to leave." She gave him a nervous smile, unwilling to explain, and afraid her emotions were easily read on her face. "I appreciate your help."

It was all she could do to keep from running to her car. She felt his concerned eyes on her back the whole way out of the barn.

As if ghosts of the past pursued her, she jumped in her car and set out with the accelerator nailed to the floor. She had to get away. She had to leave before her weakness for Davis forced her to stay.

Wearing borrowed chaps and his arms wrapped in tape, Davis grabbed the leather strips he'd fastened to the fence post and pulled. It was nearly time for his event.

He'd been awakened by a message from the ranch foreman about the arrangements for him to get back to Dallas that afternoon. It had been an eye-opener. He'd hoped and prayed that during his drive back to town with Charlie that love would somehow prevail.

But it wasn't to be.

He'd quickly learned that Charlie had already left the ranch. Too late to beg her to stay. Too late.

It had taken all the joy out of his first rodeo as a competing cowboy. As he looked into his future, all he could see was futility and emptiness.

If he had it to do over again, would he make the same decision? Having Charlie forever had been within his grasp, and he'd blown it. Totally blown it.

He had to be a first-class idiot.

He heard his name being called. Turning, he couldn't believe his eyes. "Charlie?"

He ran to join her and pulled her to his chest. "I thought you'd left."

"I did. But I came back." She stepped away from him. "I had to watch—to be here. I had to be sure you would be okay."

Davis wanted to pull her into his arms and never let go, but she kept her distance. "Thank you for coming back. It means a lot to me."

The steer roping event was announced over the loudspeakers. "I need to go to the staging area."

Charlie nodded. "I know. Be safe," her voice wavered. She gave him a sorry excuse for an encouraging smile, making his gut clench. "Make me proud, Davis."

"You'll be here when it's over?"

"This doesn't change anything." She bit her lip. "You need to hurry, Davis, or you'll miss your turn. Afterwards, I still have to go."

"But you'll watch me compete?"

She nodded.

"I will make you proud. And afterwards, we'll talk."

"No promises." She grabbed him and gave him a

fierce kiss, then pushed him on his way. "Go get your steer."

Her smile churned his insides. He was grateful she was here. It meant there was still a chance. Maybe he should take this as a sign to leave well enough alone. Maybe he shouldn't ride.

But the sounds of the rodeo called to him. The sounds of his childhood dream: to grow up to be just like his grandfather.

Reaching the staging area, he got in his place in line. The smell of horse and bull and hay filled his senses. The noise of the crowd and the announcer's voice clogged his head. The trapped boy inside him begged for just this one ride. Just let him get his steer.

Monty Joe came forward and thwapped him on the back. "You're going to do great."

"I sure hope so."

Before he knew it, his turn to mount his horse had arrived.

Fear is an amazing thing, Charlie thought as adrenaline rushed through her limbs. She tried to separate her thoughts from her body, as if by concentrating on the physical she could deny the emotional.

Davis climbed onto his horse and the chute opened. He chased after his steer. She willed her eyes to close, unwilling to watch. *Fear did that to a person,* she told herself. *Fear mocked courage.*

Forget these idiot cowboys!

Anger now replaced her fear. Anger over men willing to risk everything for a few minutes of glory. Anger at her inability to stop a risk-taking cowboy. Anger about her lack of control. Why couldn't she have meant more to Davis than his foolish need to prove that he's more macho or braver than all the others?

She heard the roar of the crowd. She prayed, *Let Davis be okay.* She threw open her eyes. Davis stood beside his steer. She checked the clock. He'd done it in an extremely short time. And he was safe.

Davis positively beamed. He blew her a kiss from the arena. Charlie's stomach somersaulted. She was going to be sick. She had to get away. The roar of the crowd buffeted her, and dizziness cloyed at her senses.

Standing, she ran out from the arena area and quickly found her car. She couldn't watch any longer. Images of her brothers, her parents and Hank filled her head. She couldn't watch another cowboy's excitement. She couldn't watch Davis do this again.

It would kill her. Because she loved him. It would kill her by inches, slowly eroding everything she was, everything she believed in. Risk was good when it meant life could be experienced, but there had to be a happy medium. With a cowboy, there were no happy mediums. Her whole life experience had taught her that.

She struggled with her seatbelt until it snapped into place. Placing her car in gear, she headed for home and safety, as if by adding physical distance between her and Davis, she'd find some measure of emotional space as well.

When Davis saw Charlie leave the arena, he realized she was leaving for good that time. He wanted to chase after her, but he'd won the buckle for the event and her brothers prevented him from leaving until he'd taken his prize.

Now the rodeo was over, and both Bobby Gray and Monty Joe stood before him, glaring.

"You should have let me go after her."

"The way I figure it," replied Bobby Gray, "she wouldn't have left if you hadn't done something wrong." His facial muscles flexed.

"What did you do?" demanded Monty Joe, taking a step closer to Davis.

"I didn't do anything. She didn't want me to compete."

"Is that all? She's a tad squeamish is all." Monty Joe laughed. "You'll have between now and the wedding to make her come around."

Davis sighed, worried about what would happen next, but he thought it best to lay his cards on the table. "There's not going to be a wedding."

Davis wasn't sure if it would work, but he'd never been a quitter and he wouldn't start now. He strode into Charlie's library as if he owned the place—as if his whole world hadn't tumbled down around his boots.

He rode the elevator to the top floor, where the research department had its offices. As the doors opened, he immediately saw Charlie behind a glass window. His heart skipped a beat.

He exited the elevator and took a step toward her. She looked beautiful, just like love personified. She also looked tired—and sad. Had he done that to her?

He stopped.

By refusing to take his calls, both at home and at work, she'd made it clear she wanted nothing to do with him. Perhaps that would be best. The past three weeks had been the longest in his life, but he'd needed them to complete his plans.

Charlie spoke into a phone receiver, a furrow wrinkling her brow. Then her eyes caught him, with a look so loving and so frightened that he realized it was too late. He was snared as surely as any rabbit caught in a trap. Not only did she own his heart, she owned his soul. If it meant a lifetime merely watching her from behind a glass window, that's what he'd do.

"He's here. Quick, tell me what to do!" Charlie's heart hammered in her throat. Her gaze settled on the bandage taped to Davis's forehead, and she wondered what had happened to him.

"Who's there?" asked Joanne.

Davis's ring, which she'd removed the day she left the Nelson Ranch, burned her chest where it hung, hidden, on a chain beneath her blouse.

She could barely breathe. Davis, despite the bandage, looked so good she wanted to throw her arms around him. Yet his mere presence threatened her in every sense of the word. She wanted to run. She wanted to hug him and never let go.

"*Him*. What am I going to do?"

"Davis is there?"

"Yes." Her voice reflected her hysteria by rising an octave but she couldn't stop watching him. Couldn't tear her eyes away from his. "What do I do now?"

"Want to know what I'd do?"

Davis took a step toward her. "I'd welcome any ideas. My brain has turned to mud."

"I'd hang up this phone . . ."

"And then what?" She couldn't think. She couldn't breathe.

"Then I'd get down on my knees and beg him to propose again."

"You're no help at all. I can't marry him." With each step Davis took, her heart beat harder and faster.

"You're an idiot, Charlie. Worse than any cowboy you've ever talked about."

"He's almost here."

He entered her office. She dropped the phone and it landed on the floor. She could hear Joanne saying, "Charlie? Charlie?" But she was unable to move. Davis was looking at her with the same look he'd given his mother that first night at the country club.

A look that screamed of love and acceptance, and oh, she was scared.

Without saying a word, Davis took her hand. She trembled at his touch. Even her teeth shook.

He lowered himself to one knee.

She was hyperventilating. She knew it. She ought to place her head between her knees. But then he spoke.

"I love you, Charlotte Susan Nelson. I love you with every fiber of my being, and I have reason to believe you love me too."

Her heart stopped. Her breathing stopped. Her mouth was parched. She couldn't move. Couldn't close it. Couldn't do anything but absorb the vision of Davis kneeling in front of her.

"Marry me. Please, Charlie, marry me."

She couldn't speak. The sound of Joanne's voice whined out of the telephone receiver. "Say yes, Charlie. Tell the man you will!"

Charlie shook her head. She couldn't. She simply couldn't.

Davis's jaw clenched. Then that stubborn, determined look that so reminded her of her brother's prize bull came over his face.

"I don't need your final answer now, Charlie. I have something to show you."

He swooped her up into his arms.

"What's happening?" asked Joanne.

As he headed toward her office door, Charlie yelled, hoping Joanne could hear, "Call 911. I'm being kidnapped!"

Davis hefted her more tightly into his arms. "Whatever it takes, Elf. Whatever it takes."

"This won't work, you know."

"The only thing I'm sure of is that you're more contrary than any mule I've had the misfortune of meeting."

Charlie crossed her arms. "I don't have to speak to you."

"Fine." Davis gave her a sly grin. "Kissing you doesn't require conversation."

"Don't even think about it," growled Charlie.

"I can't stop thinking about it." Davis helped her into his vehicle.

He'd been truck shopping. It was a bright red pickup, with a rack mounted in the rear window. She bit back a laugh when she realized the rack held branding irons rather than rifles. Talk about a one-track mind.

No matter what Davis had in mind, Charlie knew she was safe with him. He'd never force her to do anything she felt uncomfortable about. She trusted him. But she still scooched to the far right corner of the truck.

He started the engine and began driving without saying a word.

After ten minutes of highway driving, her curiosity peaked. "Where are you taking me?"

"You'll see."

"Davis."

"Yes?"

"Tell me before I scream."

He grinned. "You're one of those people who try to peek at their Christmas and birthday presents early, aren't you? Finding clever hiding places will keep me on my toes."

Charlie stuck her chin in the air, giving up on wheedling the destination out of him. She shifted to look out of the passenger window, needing time to get her wayward emotions under control.

He's a cowboy, she reminded herself. *Charlie Nelson doesn't do cowboys.* She repeated the thoughts over and over again, like a litany.

While she'd hoped her cold shoulder treatment would deter Davis from whatever wild scheme he had in mind, it wasn't working. He good-naturedly popped a country western cassette into the player and sang along, then pounded out the beat on the steering wheel while heading out of town.

Where was he taking her?

Before long, she had her answer as he pulled onto a long gravel driveway. They were miles from the highway, and although the drive hadn't taken much more than thirty minutes, the countryside was rural. Over the driveway, a white painted wrought-iron sign read, *The Dallas Branch Ranch.*

"We're almost there now." Davis pulled to a stop in front of a precious brick house.

Davis didn't say a word as she climbed from the truck to get a better look at the house. It wasn't large, but it was one of the coziest-looking homes she'd ever seen. Ivy and spring flowers cascaded from window boxes beneath every window except the main bowfront. Shrubs and violets danced in the March wind in planter boxes surrounding the house. And a weeping willow to the right side of the yard was just bursting out with buds.

"What do you think?"

"It's darling."

"I'm glad you like it." Davis smiled at her, a nervous tick vibrating in his jaw. "I bought it for us."

Charlie nearly jumped out of her skin. "Us?"

"Come around back." Davis took her hand and led her behind the house. They were at the crest of a hill, and just below them was a moderate-sized barn, a cattle shed, plus a few small outbuildings. "It's only twenty acres for now, just enough to get my feet wet in ranching."

Charlie didn't know what to say. Just behind her lay the home of her dreams, and beneath sat Davis's dreams. Was it possible to have both?

"I've got an option on more than enough acreage to make a go of things should this work out."

Charlie's mind buzzed. She couldn't think. "It sounds like you've got things well planned out."

"I hope so. I've got great consultants."

She nodded, trying to sort out the myriad of contradictory feelings bombarding her.

Just then, a pickup pulled around the back of the house. Her brothers soon emerged, then disappeared into the barn. "What are *they* doing here?"

Davis rubbed his bandaged head. "Your brothers and I reached a compromise. I've gone into partnership with them."

"Oh, no." Charlie clutched her face in her hands. "You've bonded."

"They're providing me with half a dozen calves to get started." Davis smiled reassuringly. "They know you may still be unwilling to marry me, but they also know how I feel about you. They're willing to take a chance—on me."

That was the bottom line. Her brothers could take a chance on him and she wouldn't. Why was this so hard?

"My dream of ranching won't be worth salt without you here to share it."

She started to speak but he silenced her with a look.

"I wasted ten days trying to convince myself otherwise and failed. Then I realized, that to really live, to experience life, I had to make choices and take some chances. So I'm staking my life on you loving me, too."

She brushed the tears from her eyes, unsure when they'd begun to flow, but unable to stop them from coursing down her cheeks.

He handed her a clean handkerchief he pulled from his back pocket. "What do you say? Are you willing to take a chance on my love?"

Wiping her face and blowing her nose to buy time, she tried desperately to think of one reason why she shouldn't throw herself in his arms. She loved him.

Even if their happiness was short-term, wouldn't

it be worth the cost of potentially losing him? "I don't know what to do."

Davis pulled her into his arms. "I know you don't. That's why I dragged you here, because I know exactly what you should do. Love me. Marry me."

In avoiding cowboys, had she in essence been avoiding living? Was she strong enough to marry a man who'd take risks on a daily basis? She had to be crazy, but Davis was right. She knew exactly what she had to do.

Her stomach tumbling with a sensation not unlike stepping off a cliff, she opened her mouth to say *yes*.

Davis spoke before she had the chance. "During these ten days, I've done some heavy thinking. I realized that what you were asking of me wasn't that much. It's reasonable to ask the person you love not to take unnecessary risks."

What was he saying? Was he saying they shouldn't get married after all? Or had the world gone topsy-turvy and he was now agreeing with her?

"What I want is this." Davis pointed at the ranch. "Not the competition, not the buckles, not the risk of rodeoing. Charlie, I'm a rancher, not a cowboy. I want the reality of living this life, not some fantasy of glory."

She should have known before that taking a risk was the only way to find happiness. Safety wasn't living. Security held nothing to being loved.

"I, Charlotte Susan Nelson, would be honored—no, downright thrilled—to marry you, Davis Murphy. I'm just lucky you're more stubborn than I am."

Davis lowered his lips to hers, blocking out all conscious thought. When they came up for air, Charlie no longer had a sense of place and time. All she had eyes for was the look of love on Davis's adorable face.

"You see, not all cowboys are bad. You know I'll never be bored."

"I know. I know with all my heart." Somehow, she'd been blessed enough to fall in love with the only kind of cowboy she could ever love.

A cowboy exactly like him.

"I've only got one stipulation, Charlie."

She rolled her eyes. "I might have known you'd think up something. Can't we just enjoy this moment a little longer?"

Davis laughed. "Whatever you say."

"Thanks."

"How about if I ask one small favor?"

There was no silencing the man. He was as stubborn and tenacious as any mule. She might as well humor him since it'd be the only way to shut him up. "What's the favor?"

"Don't make me wait until fall for the wedding." Davis kissed her again. "I'm certain I can't wait that long."

It was Charlie's turn to laugh. "Don't worry. I can't either." Then she threw her arms around him and knew she'd never let go.